The Old Willis Place

MARY DOWNING HAHN

The Old Willis Place

A Ghost Story

CLARION BOOKS

New York

Clarion Books
a Houghton Mifflin Company imprint
215 Park Avenue South, New York, NY 10003
Copyright © 2004 by Mary Downing Hahn

The text was set in 13.5-point Perpetua.

www.houghtonmifflinbooks.com

Printed in the U.S.A.

Library of Congress Cataloging-in-Publication Data

Hahn, Mary Downing.
The old Willis place : a ghost story / by Mary Downing Hahn.
p. cm.
Summary: Tired of the rules that have bound them ever since "the bad thing happened," twelve-year-old Diana ignores her brother's warnings and befriends the
daughter of the new caretaker, setting in motion events that lead to the release
of the spirit of an evil, crazy woman who once ruled the old Willis place.
ISBN 0-618-43018-0
[1. Ghosts—Fiction. 2. Haunted houses—Fiction. 3. Brothers and sisters—
Fiction. 4. Friendship—Fiction.] I. Title.
PZ7.H1256Ol 2004
[Fic]—dc22
2004002345

ISBN-13: 978-0-618-43018-5
ISBN-10: 0-618-43018-0

MP 10 9 8 7 6

For Ann, Tom, and Jocelyn Ingham—
who know the old Willis place far
better than I ever will
—M.D.H.

Chapter 1

"They're coming, they're coming!" My brother, Georgie, ran up the shady driveway, almost too excited to speak. "Hide, Diana! Hide!"

I didn't need to ask who was coming. Scooping up my cat, Nero, I plunged into the tangle of vines and weeds lining the drive. Georgie was right behind me. Together we squatted down and watched a pickup slowly approach, bumping over the ruts. The sun and leaves patterned the windshield, hiding the people inside. Their belongings were piled haphazardly in the truck bed, held in place with ropes. Wedged among mattresses, bed frames, chests, tables, and stacks of cardboard boxes, a big golden dog panted and lurched around, excited by the smells of the woods.

"The new caretaker," I whispered. "Who's in the truck with him?"

Beside me, Nero tensed his long black body and twitched his tail, his green eyes wide with curiosity.

Georgie was still breathing hard from running to warn

me. "A girl about your age. I couldn't see her very well, but the man got out of the truck to unlock the gate. He was tall and skinny and he was wearing baggy shorts. His legs were long and white." Georgie almost choked with laughter. "And he had big knobby knees."

I giggled. "He sounds like the heron we see at the pond."

"Yes, that's exactly what he looked like—long neck, pointed nose, and his hair stuck up in a crest." Georgie bumped against me, his shoulders shaking with laughter. "Heron Man, that's what we'll call him."

"Shh, shh," I hushed him. "The dog's looking this way."

The dog barked, but no one in the truck noticed. I imagined he barked often. Dogs are foolish. They bark so much at nothing that people don't pay attention, even when they should.

The truck passed us. I glimpsed the driver's birdy profile and suppressed a giggle. Soundlessly we followed the truck, keeping the trees and brambles between us and the lane. We knew where it was going.

The truck slowed almost to a stop as it approached the house. The old Willis place everyone called it, though its true name was Oak Hill Manor. The front lawn was a field of knee-high weeds and thistles the size of small trees. Paint peeled from the front door and wood trim. The steps and porch had rotted long ago. Shutters hung crooked from the boarded windows; some had fallen off and leaned against the house. Slates from the roof littered the yard. Two tall double chimneys tilted to the right, giving the place an unstable look, as if it might topple over at any moment in a tumble of bricks.

I wondered how much the new caretaker had been told about the old Willis place. Georgie and I had been watching the house long enough to learn quite a bit. For instance, we knew the owner, Miss Lilian Willis, had been dead for about ten years. It was common knowledge she hadn't left a will, so the county owned the property now. Workmen had patched up the house in a temporary way, covering the windows with plywood and draping the leaky roof with sheets of heavy blue plastic. They'd put chains and padlocks on the doors and posted "No Hunting, No Trespassing" signs at the gate.

They'd also hired a caretaker to live in a trailer parked near the house. He hadn't done much work or stayed long. Neither had the others the county hired, one after another, too many now to remember all their names. Maybe night noises scared them—the barking of foxes, the shrill screech of owls, the rustle of unseen deer in the woods. Maybe they didn't care for the solitude. Maybe they believed in ghosts. Or came to believe in them. At any rate, after a few months, one would leave and a week or so later another would come. Where the county found them I can't imagine. They were a sorry lot. Old and grumpy. Lazy, too.

Now we had a new caretaker to spy on. And he had a daughter. I could hardly wait to learn more about her. What books did she read? What games did she play? What did she do when she thought no one was watching? If only she could be my friend, if only—

Georgie interrupted my daydreams with a jab of his elbow. "When do you think they'll get out of that truck?" he whispered, full of impatience as usual. "Heron Man just sits there and talks and talks."

"He must be telling the girl about the house," I said. "And Miss Lilian."

Georgie cowered beside me, suddenly fearful. "Don't say that name, Diana. It's bad luck." As he spoke, he peered at the house's boarded windows. Nothing moved except the vines rippling over the walls and the shadows they made.

I shivered, knowing my brother was right. We never spoke the old woman's name out loud, just as we never went too close to her house. Miss Lilian was the snake in the garden, the witch in the gingerbread house, someone to fear even though she was dead.

At last, the truck moved on and parked next to the trailer. We scurried after it and hid in a thicket of dead vines and pokeweed. Unseen, we watched the man and his daughter get out of the truck.

As Georgie had said, the man was just as tall and scrawny as a person can be, a human heron if I'd ever seen one. His

4

shorts looked three sizes too big and so did his T-shirt. But he had a pleasant face and a nice smile.

I knew at a glance he wasn't like the other caretakers. Which made him more dangerous, I supposed. He was the sort who noticed things.

The girl was pretty, small and slender, about eleven or twelve years old. My age. Her hair hung down her back, smooth and wavy, so dark it shone with blue highlights in the sun.

The first thing the girl did was get the dog out of the truck. He was a big mutt, part golden retriever, part shepherd maybe. I couldn't tell if he was fierce or not, but he hadn't caught scent of Georgie and me yet.

"Give MacDuff some water," her father said, "but keep him tied, Lissa. I don't want him running off into the woods."

"Lissa," I murmured. It was a pretty name—a whisper, a sighing sound like a breeze blowing through a field of wheat.

I watched Lissa tie MacDuff to a tree and bring him a bowl of water. Leaving the dog lapping sloppily, she helped her father lift a shiny blue bicycle off the truck.

"A bike." Georgie nudged me. "Wouldn't you love to ride it?"

He didn't bother to hide the longing in his voice. Our bikes had disappeared a long time ago, soon after the bad thing happened. Despite the warm fall sunshine, I shivered at the memory.

"Maybe she'll leave it outside," I said, "and we can borrow it after dark for a moonlight ride."

"We could go a long way on a bike like that," Georgie said. "Miles and miles, on and on and on——"

"Yes, all the way to the gate and back," I reminded him.

He sighed and plucked a blade of grass to chew on. "I know, I know. I was just daydreaming, that's all." He sounded so sad that I was sorry I'd said anything. But I couldn't let him forget the rules.

Lissa leaned her bike against a shed. "Will it be safe here, Dad?" she asked.

"Sure," he said. "We're a mile from the road, and the gate's locked. Who'd take it?"

Georgie and I pressed our hands over our mouths to keep from laughing out loud. They'd learn soon enough what was safe and what wasn't.

"Give me a hand with some of these boxes, Lissa," her father said.

We watched them come and go, carrying things into the trailer. To Georgie the best thing was the television. What pleased me most were the books, boxes and boxes of them. It had been a long time since I'd had anything new to read. Or anyone to talk to but my brother.

Without thinking, I said, "Wouldn't it be fun to be friends with Lissa?"

Georgie stared at me, wide-eyed with shock. "Friends? We can't be friends with her. You know that, Diana."

I gazed past him at the trailer. I'd never wanted to break the rules before. Not once. For as long as I'd known what we could and couldn't do, I'd accepted the rules completely. I'd stayed hidden, I'd never gone beyond the gate at the end of the drive, I'd kept away from Miss Lilian's house. But now, for the first time, I was tempted.

I looked at Georgie. "How can it hurt to have a friend?"

He scowled. "I can't ride that bike past the gate, and you can't have a friend. We're not allowed."

Suddenly angry, I pinched his arm. "What can happen if just one little time—"

Georgie pulled away and rubbed his arm. "You'd better not talk like that," he whispered. "You'll ruin everything."

"Ruin everything?" I glared at him. "It seems to me everything's already ruined."

Without answering, Georgie moved deeper into the shade. Behind him, the sun shone on a field where corn once grew. My brother and the trees were dark against the brilliance.

"Where are you going?" I was torn between following him and staying where I was, watching Lissa and her father.

"Nowhere." Then he was gone.

Sometimes Georgie was such a baby. I hadn't really hurt him. One little pinch. He deserved it for being such a spoilsport. Who did he think he was, telling me what to do? I was older than he was. He had no right to boss me around. If I wanted to break the rules, he couldn't stop me. So I stayed put, with Nero beside me.

Through the trailer's open windows, I heard Lissa and her father debating where to put their things. I'd been inside and knew how small it was—two bedrooms, a tiny bathroom, a small kitchen, an eating area, and a living room. It was good they didn't have much furniture.

After a while, Lissa's father took the dog inside. I heard Lissa showing him his new sleeping place. "Right here in Daddy's room," she said. "I wish you could sleep in my room, but it's not big enough."

I waited a while, but when Lissa didn't come back outside, I slipped into the woods to find my brother. He'd gone to our hideout, an old shed almost covered by the wild grape, honeysuckle, and brambles growing around and over it.

When he saw me, he frowned. "What do you want?"

"I'm sorry I pinched you." I squatted beside him on the shed's dirt floor. "But you made me mad."

Georgie rubbed his arm. "You hurt me. Your fingernails are sharp."

I looked at my nails. Georgie was right. I'd let them grow long and sharp like claws. I flexed my fingers and made scratching motions like a cat. "*Pfssst*," I hissed at him.

Georgie edged away as if he didn't quite trust me. "You won't really break the rules, will you?"

"I'm sick to death of those stupid rules," I said. "Aren't you?"

Georgie shrugged and picked up a stick. I watched him practice writing his name in the dirt. "I don't want to get in trouble," he said. "I don't want to be punished. Things could be worse, you know."

I sighed. It was hopeless to argue with Georgie. "But don't you miss friends and—"

Georgie pressed his warm hand over my mouth. "We promised not to talk about those things."

I pulled away from him. "But—"

"We promised, Diana!" Georgie got to his feet and covered his ears with his hands. If I said one more word, he'd run off again.

"All right," I said, "all right. Forget Lissa." Which of course I had no intention of doing.

Georgie grinned in relief. "Let's go down to the creek and catch minnows. It's cool and shady there."

I followed him across a field grown wild with milkweed and goldenrod. Purple-crowned thistles shot skyward. Bees droned around us, eager to get the last of the nectar before winter set in.

We saw a vixen and her kits playing in a hollow near their den. They watched us pass without running for cover. We meant them no harm and they knew it.

"You'd better be careful," Georgie called to the foxes. "A

new caretaker has come. The last one set traps, remember?"

"And the one before that had a shotgun," I added.

The vixen pricked up her ears as if she intended to take heed of our warning. The kits tumbled about her feet, yelping and nipping at each other, too young to listen. What was danger? What were rules? They had no idea.

We passed a family of rabbits grazing on clover; a groundhog; a deer and her fawn. We told them what we'd told the foxes. It was silly, I supposed, but it made us feel better. We knew how to spring traps and ruin a hunter's aim, but we had no idea if we'd need our skills this time. We hadn't learned the ways of the new caretaker. But we'd find out, the way we always did—by watching and following . . . and waiting.

Chapter 2

When it was almost dark, Georgie and I sneaked back to the trailer. No matter how risky it was, we couldn't stay away. This time it was the smell of food cooking that drew us to the edge of the woods.

Lissa and her father were sitting at a sagging old picnic table that had been in the yard as long as the trailer. The wood was silver gray with age. Every caretaker who'd lived on the farm had carved his initials in the top. Georgie and I had carved ours more than once, using a jackknife we'd stolen from Mr. Wagner, one of the first caretakers. As Georgie had said, the old man could always get another one.

While hamburgers sizzled on a grill, Lissa sliced tomatoes. MacDuff watched eagerly, hoping a burger would come his way. Barely containing his appetite, he inched forward, making a little squeaky crying sound.

"Get back, MacDuff," Lissa's dad said.

MacDuff cried a little harder but backed off.

"Lie down, boy."

MacDuff obeyed, but he never took his eyes off those burgers.

Neither did Georgie.

With watering mouths, we watched Lissa and her father eat their dinner. I was glad to see they gave MacDuff his very own burger. But I wished, oh, how I wished, they'd give Georgie and me one, too. It would be so lovely to sink our teeth into hot juicy food again.

But the rules were the rules. They had to be obeyed. No burgers for us. Not tonight, not ever.

Heron Man smiled at Lissa. "Well, what do you think of our new home?"

"It's kind of spooky," she said slowly. "We've never lived in a place like this. No neighbors. Just woods and fields and that scary old house. I don't know if I'm going to like it or not."

"It will be a great place to write, though," her father said. "I might actually finish my novel here."

Lissa frowned. "What am I supposed to do while you sit at your computer?"

"You'll have your schoolwork," he said. "And three hundred acres of land to explore. You and MacDuff will have a lovely time."

"How about friends? I'll never meet anybody way out here." She leaned across the table. "If I could go to school, real school, I'd—"

Heron Man shook his head. "You'll get a much better education at home. School grinds kids down, destroys their minds and their imaginations. Makes them into conformists, unable to think for themselves—"

"Okay, okay!" Lissa got to her feet. "I've heard it all before." Gathering her plate and glass, she went inside. *Bang!* went the door.

Heron Man sat at the table for a while. By now it was too dark to see his face, just the sharp outline of his nose and his crest of hair. In the kitchen, Lissa ran water in the sink and began washing dishes with a lot of clattering.

Georgie nudged me. "What's wrong with her? She should be happy she doesn't have to go to school."

I sighed, too embarrassed to tell him how much I missed school myself—not arithmetic or geography or social studies, but reading and drawing and playing with my friends at recess. I missed my favorite teacher, Miss Perry, and my best friend, Jane, and a red-haired boy named Stephen. I missed jump rope and dodge ball and field trips. I even missed the cafeteria food.

Heron Man gathered his dishes and went inside. Through the kitchen window, I saw him give Lissa a kiss on the cheek. "There's a YMCA not far from here," he said. "I'll sign you up for gymnastics. Would you like that?"

Lissa gave him a hug, and they finished the dishes together. When they'd dried the last fork, Heron Man said, "Shall we see if the television works?"

"TV," Georgie whispered, "oh, let them watch TV. I've missed it since Mr. Potter left. He kept the TV on all night long. Remember? We could see and hear everything."

I smiled, remembering the fun we'd had watching TV through the window while Mr. Potter dozed in his armchair. Sometimes Georgie sneaked inside and changed channels with the remote. Mr. Potter snored away, never suspecting a thing. Finally, Georgie decided to steal the remote to save himself the trouble of climbing through the window every night.

When he woke up, Mr. Potter noticed the remote's disappearance and wasted hours searching for it, cursing up a storm the whole time. Then Georgie got the bright idea to change channels while Mr. Potter was awake. Sometimes he turned the volume up; sometimes he turned it down; sometimes he'd switch the TV off, then back on. I couldn't help feeling a little sorry for Mr. Potter.

Not too long after Georgie stole the remote, Mr. Potter quit. We heard him tell the property manager the solitude was driving him insane. He was going to stop drinking, he said, and straighten his life out. Georgie and I felt good about helping Mr. Potter reform.

Lissa's answer disappointed Georgie. "I think I'll just go to bed and read for a while," she said. "I'm tired, Daddy."

He yawned. "I'm pretty done in myself. We've had a big day."

The kitchen light went off and the bathroom light came on. In a few moments, the light in the small bedroom came on, too.

Without a word, Georgie and I sneaked across the yard to Lissa's room. We'd peeked in the windows many times before, often with pranks in mind. To make things easier, we'd hidden cinder blocks in strategic places. Standing on them, we could look in any window except the one in the bathroom, which was higher than the others. Of course, we wouldn't have looked in the bathroom even if we could have. People deserve some privacy.

Lissa was already in bed. The grumpy old men caretakers had used her room for storage, but now it was clean and neat. A green and yellow rag rug covered most of the old linoleum tile. A small desk, a narrow bookcase, and a white dresser with a mirror were crammed into the tiny space, along with Lissa's bed, painted white to match the dresser. She'd made a little nest of pillows and quilts and stuffed animals, and she looked cozy and comfortable snuggled into it, a book propped up on her knees.

After a while, Georgie nudged me. "Let's go for a ride on her bike."

We climbed down quietly from the cinder block and ran silently across the yard to the shed. The bike leaned against the wall, its chrome handlebars bright in the moonlight.

"Do you remember how to ride?" Georgie whispered.

"Of course." I walked the bike to the long dirt driveway leading away from the house. "Wait here. I'll go first."

"It was my idea," Georgie said. "I should go first."

"This bike is different from your old Schwinn. It has gears and hand brakes like the Raleigh I used to have. Let me try it first and then I can show you how everything works."

Georgie scowled and stuffed his hands in his pockets. "It's not fair. You aren't the queen of the world."

"No, not of the whole world." I straddled Lissa's bike. "Just the queen of Oak Hill Manor."

With that I pushed off and left Georgie behind. Ahead of me, the drive tunneled between massive oaks, dark with shadows, but lit here and there with patches of moonlight. The bike bounced over ruts. The cool night breeze blew in my face, bringing with it the smells of damp earth and fallen leaves. Exhilarated by speed, I hunched over the handlebars and pedaled hard. I imagined myself riding around the world, flying to the moon, coasting down the Milky Way. Like Georgie, I yearned to escape—to leave Oak Hill Manor forever.

Five deer surprised me. They stood in the middle of the drive, their eyes on me, unsure what to do. I swerved around them as they dashed into the woods, graceful as gazelles. Somehow I managed to control the bike, but my dream of flying vanished into the shadows with the deer.

The drive emerged from the trees into a grassy area. Just ahead was the locked gate and its "No Trespassing," "Private

Property," "Keep Out" signs. Beyond was the road—and the rest of the world.

I laid the bike down in the weeds and went to the fence. Hidden in the underbrush, I watched the cars speed by, their headlights sweeping over me. Every year there was more traffic, more people, more houses. Where fields and woods had once been, homes had sprung up. I could see their lights across the highway.

Suddenly, Georgie was beside me. "You said you'd come right back!"

I turned to him. "Don't you wonder where all those people are going? Look at them, just driving and driving."

"I wish we were in one of those cars, going far, far away," Georgie said. "To California, maybe. Wouldn't you love to see the Pacific Ocean?"

I patted his shoulder. "Yes, but—"

Georgie's smile faded and he leaned against the fence, watching the headlights go by. "Don't say it," he said sadly. "I know, I know."

"Hey," I said, "it's your turn to ride the bike."

Turning my back to the road and the cars, I picked up the bike and held it steady for Georgie. His legs weren't quite long enough, so he had to stand up to pedal.

"Don't shift the gears," I told him. "They work fine just the way they are. If you need the brakes, squeeze these." I put his hands on the levers. "But don't squeeze hard. If you stop too fast, you'll go right over the handlebars."

As he started to pedal back toward the house, I called after him, "Go slow at first. Get used to the feel of it. Your Schwinn was much heavier."

"Don't boss me," Georgie said. "I know how to ride a bike."

"And watch out for deer," I added. "I almost hit one."

This time he ignored me. Wobbling from side to side, he pedaled into the dark tunnel of trees. I ran after him, but he was soon out of sight. A few seconds later, I heard the bike's bell, followed by a loud crash and my brother's cry.

By the time I found Georgie, he'd righted the bicycle. "There was a fox in the drive," he said tearfully. "I missed him, but I smashed into that tree."

Georgie hadn't hurt himself, but the bike's front wheel was twisted and the tire was flat. "Nobody can ride it now." He gave the bike a kick. "Flimsy old thing."

If he hadn't looked so upset, I would have pinched him for ruining our moonlight bike rides when they'd barely begun. "Why couldn't you have been more careful?"

"I'm sorry," he mumbled.

I yanked the bike away from him. "Now what do we do?"

"Put it back where it was," he suggested. "Maybe they won't notice right away."

I shook my head. "We'll hide it. They'll think someone stole it."

Georgie brightened. "Maybe Lissa's dad will buy her a new one."

"Maybe." Pushing the bike ahead of me, I followed a deer trail deep into the woods. When I came to the creek, I shoved the bike down the bank and watched it splash into the water. It came to rest behind a clump of pokeberries. No one would find it there.

Without another word, we left the bike where it had fallen and headed for home.

THE DIARY OF LISSA MORRISON

Dear Diary,

Is this how you start? I never kept a diary before, so I'm not sure. Up till now I thought my life was too boring to think about, let alone write about, but that's changing. This is the second day Dad and I have spent here, and already strange things are happening.

First of all, the old Willis house is the creepiest place you ever saw. It's got to be haunted. Dad says the old lady who owned it was really eccentric, maybe even crazy. Anyway, she died in the house—in the front parlor, where she slept because she got too old to climb the steps to her bedroom. She lay there dead for a week before anyone found her. Ugh.

It seems like the perfect setup for a ghost, don't you think? She died there—all alone. Think about it. I can almost see her, can't you? A weird old lady, white hair, scary face, roaming around from room to room, up and down the steps, watching, waiting—oooh, I'm scaring myself.

Do you believe in ghosts, Dear Diary? Dad definitely doesn't. I talked to him after dinner about Miss Willis—that's the old lady's name—and I asked him if he thought she haunted the house. He laughed. I hate it when he laughs at me. Like he thinks I'm silly. Or dumb maybe.

If my mother was here, I know she wouldn't laugh—but she died when I was so little I can hardly remember her. Someday I'll write more about how much I miss her, but I don't want to make myself feel sad. So I will just say I wish she was here right now and we were sitting close together reading a book or something.

I know this sounds odd, Dear Diary, so don't tell anyone, but I'd love to see a ghost—just to know for sure they exist. I wouldn't be scared. At least, I don't think I'd be. How could a ghost actually hurt you? They're just ectoplasm or something, not solid.

Maybe it's because of my mother; maybe that's why I wonder so much about what happens when you die and where you go and if you can stay on earth for a while. I'd really like to know.

Now here's something else to tell you, something different. Not supernatural but scarier in a way because it's real. The first day we came to the farm, there was someone in the woods spying on us. Kids maybe. I'm sure of it. I could feel them watching me. I swear my scalp prickled. I had the same feeling while we were eating dinner last night—they were back, spying again.

I told Dad, but he says it's my imagination. I'm in a new place, I'm not used to woods all around, I hear birds and squirrels and think they're people. The way he talks, you'd think I didn't have an ounce of sense.

Maybe I should give Dad some of my spare imagination. It might help him finish that book so he can get a better job and we can live in a house with a yard and neighbors and I can go to school and have friends—instead of spies in the woods.

But that's not all—someone stole my bike last night. Dad can't blame that on birds or squirrels! We searched all over, but there's not a sign of it. My beautiful new blue bike is really and truly gone.

Dad called the police and they came out and talked to us. They said teenagers sometimes sneak onto the property and most likely that's who took my bike. When I told them I thought someone was spying on us, one of the policemen said it must have been the same kids who stole my bike. They live in a development just across the highway from the farm. The police have had trouble with them trespassing before.

The other policeman shook his head. "Funny things happen out here," he said. "None of the caretakers stay long. Place gives them the jitters, they say. Some of them claim it's haunted by the old lady who used to live here. Her and the poor—"

The first policeman coughed and said, "We'd better get going, Novak. We've got other business."

I had the funniest feeling he didn't want us to hear what Officer Novak was about to say. In case you haven't noticed, that's how it always is with adults—just when someone starts telling the interesting stuff, someone else shuts him up. I glanced at Dad, hoping he'd ask him what he was talking about, but he was watching MacDuff chase a squirrel.

Officer Novak jingled his keys and looked at me. "Don't go too far from the trailer," he said. "There's no telling who might be hanging out in the woods. And stay away from the old house."

"I hear there's a bunch of snakes in the cellar," the first policeman said. "And the floorboards are rotten in some of the rooms."

The two of them got in the police car. "Keep your eye out," the first one told Dad. "If you see anything suspicious, give us a call."

Officer Novak looked at me as if something was worrying him, but all he said was, "That's a real nice dog you've got."

We watched them drive away. I was hoping they'd turn their lights and siren on, but they didn't. I guess they only do that in movies.

So now Dad thinks I might have been right about kids hiding in the woods, spying and stealing stuff. Three hundred acres—there must be a ton of hiding places on this farm.

I'm going to look for them. If I find them, I'll tell them to give my bike back—or else they'll end up in jail or juvenile detention. They can't scare me. And neither can Miss Willis.

Well, I've written so much my hand hurts, so I think I'll stop and read in bed for a while. It sure is dark outside. Not a streetlight. Not a house light. Not even a headlight going past.

Your friend, Lissa

P.S. I'm going to call you Dee Dee. It makes you seem more like a real pen pal.

Chapter 3

The sound of falling rain woke Georgie and me. It pinged on the shed's tin roof like someone was beating on it with drumsticks. Nero curled beside me, purring, happy to be warm and dry. Georgie looked less happy.

"Rain. I hate rain." He snuggled deeper under his blankets, as if he meant to sleep until the sun came out. "I wish we had a new book to read."

I looked at the pile of old books we'd borrowed from Miss Lilian. "How about *Clematis*? We haven't read that for a long time."

"I said a *new* book. I'm sick of those old ones. Especially *Clematis*. It's a silly girly girl story." Georgie pulled the blankets over his head. "Besides, I hate sappy endings."

I yanked the covers back and laughed at his scowling face. "Tonight we'll borrow a book from Lissa," I promised. "She has a whole shelf full of them. Surely she won't miss one or two."

"I want a story right now," Georgie mumbled. "Tell me the one about us."

"But it always makes you cry."

"Tell it anyway."

I sighed and stretched out on my back beside him. "Once there was a little boy named Georgie," I began. "He had a big sister named Diana. They lived in a little house on a big farm with their mother and father. It wasn't their farm. It belonged to Mr. and Mrs. Willis, but Georgie and Diana could play anywhere they wanted. Inside and outside."

"Upstairs and downstairs," Georgie added. "Diana and Georgie were so happy."

"Most of the time," I said.

"*All* of the time," Georgie insisted. "They rode bicycles— their very own bicycles. And they had lots of books to read. They had warm beds. And food, delicious food. Ice cream, candy, cake, and cookies, all they could eat."

Lulled by the rain into a dreamy state like Georgie's, I said, "Devil's food cake was their favorite. And chocolate chip cookies still warm from the oven, all gooey and sweet. Mother read to them every night and Daddy took them fishing in the pond."

"And Diana played the piano every single day." Georgie snuggled closer. "Those were the best times ever."

"Except for Miss Lilian." I was sorry the moment the old woman's name popped out of my mouth. It hung in the air for a long moment, a dark cloud over our heads, a curse nothing could dispel.

Georgie drew away from me and covered his ears. "Stop, Diana! Don't tell the bad part."

"But you said—"

"I've changed my mind." Throwing his covers back, Georgie got to his feet and dashed out into the rain.

"Georgie!" I ran to the shed's door and peered after him, but he was already out of sight. "Come back," I called. "You'll get soaked."

There was no answer, just the sound of the rain and the wind stripping the trees, filling the air with ragged yellow leaves.

"Georgie," I called again. Still no answer. He'd probably stay away all day, holed up in one of his secret hideouts.

I stepped back from the sheets of water pouring off the roof. If I hadn't mentioned Miss Lilian, my brother and I would still be telling tales about the old days, amusing ourselves while the rain fell and the wind blew. Now Georgie was gone and I was alone.

To keep myself from thinking about the bad part, I rummaged through our pile of moldering belongings until I found *Clematis*. I made a snug nest of blankets for myself, not nearly as cozy as Lissa's soft, clean bed, and opened the book. Just inside the front cover, spidery handwriting proclaimed, "This book belongs to me, Lilian Willis."

Well, not anymore, I thought. It's mine now.

As the wind murmured through the cracks in the shed's

walls, I could almost hear my mother's voice reading to me the way she once did. It would be lovely to cuddle up beside her while Georgie sat nearby, building block towers and pretending not to listen. We'd have hot chocolate by the fire, and slabs of devil's food cake. So warm, so cozy, rain falling outside, firelight glowing inside.

Drowsy-eyed, I let the book drop to my side. Snuggling deeper under the covers, I drifted into dreams of happy days with Mother and Daddy.

I slept most of the day, but Georgie didn't come back till after dark. Nero heard him before I did. He leapt from his place beside me, his ears pricked up, and ran to the door to welcome my brother.

"Where have you been?" I asked him.

Georgie flopped down on his pile of blankets, shaking off water like a dog. "You should have come with me. I went to the trailer and I—"

"Did you see Lissa?"

"I saw her and her father." He paused a second. "*And* the police. Mr. Morrison—that's their last name, I heard the police say it—called them about the bike. One cop said kids from town probably stole it, but the other said strange things happen here. He told them how none of the caretakers stay long. How some of them spread stories about ghosts and other weird stuff."

"*Boooooo,*" I moaned in a ghostly voice. "*Boooooo!*"

We laughed, knowing exactly who was to blame for the caretakers' abrupt departures.

"What did Lissa's father say?" I asked.

"He just laughed, but Lissa told the police she's sure people are hiding in the woods. She feels them watching her. The policeman said they were the same kids who stole the bike. He thinks they live in those houses across the highway."

"Was Lissa scared?"

Georgie shook his head. "She seemed more mad than anything. If you ask me, she's kind of spoiled. You know, only child and all that. I bet she always gets her own way."

I picked up Nero and rubbed his head with my chin. The cat purred, but I frowned. What did Georgie know about Lissa? He was a boy, after all. He didn't know anything about girls. Lissa was nice, I could tell. She'd be a good friend, if only—if only, if only, if only.

"The policeman warned Lissa to stay close to the trailer and not to go to Miss Lilian's house," Georgie went on. "If Lissa and her father see anything suspicious, he wants them to call right away."

I lay on my back with Nero on my chest, purring so loudly I could feel his whole body vibrating. "I'm glad Mr. Morrison doesn't believe in ghosts," I said. "It would be awful if he quit. He and Lissa are much more interesting than the grumpy old men who usually take the job."

Georgie shrugged. "He sure was mad about the bike."

"I'm mad about the bike, too."

"I said I was sorry." Georgie rubbed his hair dry with a blanket and took off his wet clothes. In a pair of baggy pants that used to belong to Mr. Potter and a sweatshirt he'd found in the woods, Georgie looked smaller than ever.

I got to my feet, tired of being indoors. "Let's see what they're doing now."

The night air was cold and thick with mist. The rain had stopped, but the trees were dripping and the ground was wet. We mucked through the woods and across the field. In the gloom, we saw the trailer's cheerful lighted windows.

Lissa and her father were in the living room playing checkers. MacDuff lay beside Lissa, his nose on his paws, sound asleep.

"We should borrow the checkers, too," Georgie whispered. "I'm tired of playing with stones and acorns. Just think, a real board instead of squares scratched in the dirt."

I put my finger to my lips. "Hush. Do you want to wake MacDuff?"

We watched Mr. Morrison win the game by capturing Lissa's last king. "Time for bed, kiddo," he said.

"Just wait till tomorrow night." Lisa smiled and kissed him good night. "I'll beat you."

"We'll see about that." Her father got to his feet and turned off the light.

Georgie and I sneaked around to Lissa's window and hopped up on the cinder block. She was already in bed, reading. I squinted hard at the title. *Lassie Come-Home*—one of my favorites. I longed to read it again. I'd begged Daddy to let me have a collie just like Lassie, a dog who would love me best of all and be loyal and true. But he'd said no. Miss Lilian wouldn't allow a dog on her property. It might frighten her cats.

Georgie made a slight noise, and Lissa looked straight at the window. We ducked down.

"Be still," I whispered. "She almost saw us."

The next time I raised my head, Lissa was reading again. Finally, she yawned, closed the book, and laid it on the table beside her bed.

When she turned off her light, Georgie nudged me. "Should I sneak in and get the book now?"

I shook my head. "Give her time to fall sound asleep."

"Let's see what her father's doing," Georgie suggested. "His light's still on."

We crept to the other side of the trailer. "Where's Mac-Duff?" I whispered to Georgie.

He climbed up on the cinder block ahead of me. "In here," he whispered.

Sure enough, there was MacDuff, curled up in a dog nest as cozy as Lissa's bed. Mr. Morrison sat at his desk, working on his computer. It was the first one we'd ever seen, except in television ads. While we watched, words formed themselves into sentences and paragraphs on the screen. Like magic, I thought.

"He must be working on his novel," I whispered. "I wonder what it's about."

"We could borrow his computer and read it." Georgie grinned. "I bet the novel's boring, but it would be fun to have a computer."

"I think you need electricity to make one work."

"Too bad," Georgie muttered.

After Mr. Morrison quit for the night, we returned to Lissa's window. Georgie lifted the screen quietly. He'd gotten very good at borrowing, much better than I had.

Cautiously I followed him inside. He could have taken the book by himself, but I wanted a closer look at Lissa's room. While Georgie waited impatiently, I examined her stuffed animals, her books, the pictures on the walls.

I pointed to a photograph in a silver frame. "Look, Georgie," I whispered, "that must be her mother. She looks just like Lissa."

Georgie picked up the photograph and studied it. "I wonder what happened to her," he said. "Do you think she died?"

Saddened by the thought, I shook my head. "Maybe they got divorced. Lots of people do that now." Another useful bit I'd picked up watching TV.

But Georgie's interest had been caught by something else. Bending over Lissa, he carefully lifted the teddy bear lying beside her head and cradled it in his arms. "It's just like the bear Miss Lilian took away from me," he said. "She said I stole Alfie, but Mrs. Willis gave him to me. Remember how I cried and cried?"

Just then Lissa sighed in her sleep and rolled from her side to her back. Scared of waking her, I grabbed *Lassie Come-Home* and headed for the window, with Georgie right behind me.

We must have made more noise than we'd thought, because MacDuff started barking before we'd crossed the yard. We heard Mr. Morrison yell at the dog to be quiet. Lissa called out from her room, and the outside light flooded the yard.

Without waiting to see what would happen next, we fled into the woods. It wasn't until we were safely home that I noticed Georgie had brought the bear with him. He fell asleep that night holding it as tightly as he'd once held Alfie. I hadn't seen him look so happy in a long time.

THE DIARY OF LISSA MORRISON

Dear Dee Dee,

Something even more scary has happened. While I was asleep last night, someone came in my room and stole Tedward and Lassie Come-Home. *Dad says I must be mistaken, I just forgot where I put them—but I know Tedward was on my pillow; I sleep with him every night. My book was on the table beside my bed. When I woke up, they were both gone.*

I bet the same kids who stole my bike took my bear and my book. They have a lot of nerve to come into my room while I'm sleeping. They could have murdered me! How can I ever sleep in my bed again? I'll have to keep MacDuff in my room to protect me.

Oh, Dee Dee, I don't know what I'll do without Tedward. He's my most special toy, my favorite, the one I love best of all. My mother gave him to me when I was five years old, not long before she died. I've slept with him ever since. Now he's been kidnapped and I want him back! What do those kids want with a little brown bear? I love him so much.

Dad says Tedward and my book will turn up, but I doubt it. I wonder what they'll steal next. I hope they take something that belongs to him. His computer maybe. Then he'll know how it feels.

If only Dad would fix the lock on my window. But oh, no, he's too busy working on his book to do anything like that. He won't even help me search for those kids. He says they're long gone, but he called the police and reported it, just the same.

If they dare to come back, I'll sic MacDuff on them. He'll give them a bite they won't forget!

Oh, Dee Dee—I wish you were real and could write back to me and tell me what you think. I feel like I'm talking to myself, going on and on, writing letters nobody will ever read.

Well, that's all for now. I guess I'll take MacDuff for a walk. And keep my eyes peeled, as people say—which is a very weird expression when you think about it. Eyes peeled like grapes. Ugh.

See ya later—

Your friend, Lissa

Chapter 4

The next morning Georgie and I made ourselves comfortable in our favorite tree, and I began reading *Lassie Come-
Home* to him. Nero climbed to a high branch and stretched
himself along its length like a panther surveying his king-
dom. He dozed lightly, as cats do, swinging his tail from
time to time to show he was keeping an eye on us.

The first thing I noticed about Lissa's book was that the
pictures were exactly the same as I remembered. There was
Lassie, sitting at the gate, waiting for her boy, Joe. And the
words were the same, too. "'Everyone in Greenall Bridge
knew Sam Carraclough's Lassie,'" I read. "'In fact, you
might say that she was the best-known dog in the village—
and for three reasons.'"

I leaned against the tree's rough bark and smiled at
Georgie. "Isn't that a great beginning?"

"Go on," Georgie said. "What happens next? What are
the three reasons?"

I read the first three chapters. I'd meant to stop after one,
to make the book last longer, but Georgie insisted I keep

going. Like me, he was furious when Sam Carraclough sold Lassie and even more furious when the dog was mistreated by Hynes, the evil kennel man. He finally agreed to let me stop for the day when it seemed Lassie was about to escape from the kennel and meet Joe at school as she always did.

"Now Joe will get to keep Lassie," Georgie said with confidence. "The duke will see that Lassie loves Joe too much to take her away from him. And he'll fire Hynes."

Of course, Georgie was wrong. It wouldn't be much of a story if everyone got to be happy right away.

I hid Lissa's book in a special hole in the tree trunk where we kept other things—the TV remote, plus a jackknife and a ball of string we'd also borrowed from Mr. Potter, and a cigarette lighter and a flashlight we'd borrowed from Mr. Allesandro. I suppose that sounds bad, but they were all things we thought we might need someday. It wasn't as if we had a choice. What are people to do if they have no money?

With Nero at our heels, as faithful as a dog, we made our way through the fields and woods to the trailer. Even Georgie couldn't stay away.

Lissa was sitting on the steps. MacDuff lay by her side, panting in the fall heat. Mr. Morrison was inside, writing. Every now and then, I heard him swear. Georgie giggled at the language the man chose to express himself, but Lissa paid no attention to her father. I guessed she was used to his way of talking.

Georgie poked my side. "Do you think Mr. Morrison puts words like that in his book?"

"I hope not."

"I could borrow a few pages," Georgie offered. "And you could read them to me."

I shook my head impatiently. "It's a book for adults," I said. "And probably boring—even with cussing in it."

Georgie caught a grasshopper, something practice had made him good at, and then let it go. "Lissa writes, too," he said, "in a little book."

"Her diary, probably," I guessed.

"I bet she writes about us—the spies and thieves in the woods," Georgie said. "Wouldn't you love to read what she thinks of us? It would be easy to borrow it."

Even though I would have loved to know Lissa's thoughts, I shook my head. "Diaries are secret books. You put your deepest thoughts and most private feelings in them, things you don't want anyone else to know."

I glanced at Lissa. The sun shone on her dark hair. "I used to have a diary, but I filled it up a long time ago. It had a lock," I told Georgie. "I kept the key on a chain around my neck."

"That flimsy lock didn't stop me." Georgie edged away, ready to run. "I know all about Stephen Jenkins and the dimple in his chin and how he asked you to be his girl-friend. And you let him kiss you at the sixth-grade picnic."

Forgetting about Lissa, I jumped up to chase Georgie, but

he was gone like a flash. The two of us made so much noise Lissa got to her feet and stared across her yard at the woods.

"Thieves," she called. "You'd better bring my stuff back! My father called the police and they're after you."

MacDuff ran toward our hiding place, with Lissa right behind him, as mad as any girl I've ever seen.

Georgie had already disappeared, but I wasn't fast enough. I pressed myself against a tree trunk, hoping the sunlight and shadows would camouflage me. She'd called me a thief. Me, a thief. Didn't she know the difference between stealing and borrowing?

Just when I was sure MacDuff would find me, Nero came to my rescue. Making a loud rustling sound, he leapt out of the bushes right under MacDuff's nose. The dog forgot about me and ran after Nero. In a few bounds, the cat scrambled up a tree. Well out of MacDuff's reach, he arched his back and hissed at the dog.

"MacDuff! MacDuff!" Lissa tugged at the dog's collar, trying to pull him away from the tree. She was so close I could smell the shampoo she used, as sweet as honeysuckle. If it hadn't been for Nero, she would have seen me.

Mr. Morrison opened the door and stuck his head out. "What's all the commotion?" he yelled. "Has MacDuff treed a raccoon or something?"

"It's a big black cat," Lissa cried. "He's way up high in the tree. What if he can't get down?"

Mr. Morrison crossed the yard and grabbed MacDuff's collar. "Sit! Be quiet!"

MacDuff sat as commanded and stopped barking. Mr. Morrison peered up at Nero. The cat lashed his tail and growled. With his fur puffed up, he looked twice as big as normal, almost the size of a panther.

"It's a feral cat," Mr. Morrison said. "It can take care of itself."

"He's not feral," Lissa insisted. "He belongs to someone, I can tell. See how nice and shiny his coat is?"

"Mr. Maloney told me Miss Willis had dozens of cats," her dad said. "After she died, they ran off into the woods and went wild. I imagine there are hundreds of them out there."

"Can't you get him down, Dad?"

"With my luck, I'd fall out of the tree and break my neck." He patted Lissa's arm. "I'll take MacDuff inside. Don't worry. When the cat sees it's safe, he'll come down."

Lissa watched her father walk away with the dog. Then she looked up at Nero. "I used to have a black cat just like you, but he died last year. He was very old."

Nero began edging backward along the tree limb. Slowly he inched down the trunk. His claws made a scratching sound on the rough bark.

"Good boy," Lissa crooned as he descended, "good boy."

When Nero was low enough, Lissa lifted him from the tree and cuddled him in her arms.

"Would you like to be my cat? I'll keep you safe from MacDuff," she promised. "You can sleep on my bed at night. I'll feed you cream and sardines. And I'll call you Aladdin, like my old cat."

Nero gazed at Lissa as if he were considering her offer. I felt a twinge of jealousy. Suppose he decided to belong to Lissa? No more mice and shrews and moles, no more cold nights in the shed.

But no. In a flash, Nero jumped out of Lissa's arms. Stretching his slender body with each bound, he ran past my hiding place as if he had urgent matters to attend to. It might be a mouse hiding under a leaf, a squirrel twitching its tail on a tree trunk, a blue jay calling from a bramble bush. Away he went, ever alert, ever curious.

"Aladdin, Aladdin," Lissa called. "Come back. Kitty, kitty, kitty . . ."

For a moment I thought she was going to follow Nero and find me, but instead, she stood where she was and watched the spot in the woods where Nero had vanished, her face sad. I guessed she hoped he'd come back.

When that didn't happen, she sighed and returned to the steps. She picked up her notebook and her pen and began to write.

Before long, Mr. Morrison came to the door with Mac-Duff. "Do me a favor, Liss. Take MacDuff for a walk. He needs some exercise."

Lissa laid her diary on the step and set off across the yard. MacDuff bounded ahead, sniffing and searching the way dogs do.

"Where's she going?"

I spun around to face Georgie. "Don't ever sneak up on me like that again! You scared me half to death!"

"Sorry." Georgie's little smirk told me he wasn't one bit sorry.

"Let's follow her," I suggested, "and find out."

As usual, Georgie and I stayed in the deep shadows near the edge of the woods. Lissa and MacDuff walked in the sunlight. The dog ran in circles around the girl, sniffing the weeds, the bushes, the trees. Hundreds of grasshoppers leapt out of his way, but he didn't seem to be interested in them.

Trailing behind her dog, Lissa walked slowly toward Miss Lilian's house—just where she'd been told not to go. She must be a rule breaker, I thought. I glanced at Georgie. Maybe I'd break a few rules myself.

At the front steps, Lissa stopped and stared up at the double doors, secured with a rusty chain and padlock.

Georgie gripped my arm. "She's too close," he whispered. "What if she—"

"We have to stop her." I took a step toward the house, but Georgie tightened his hold on me.

"No. You can't let her see you!"

"But she might be in danger—"

"We can't do anything," Georgie insisted. "Besides, Lissa's not the one she wants."

Reluctantly I stepped back into the shade, unseen, unheard. Lissa was new to Oak Hill Manor. She knew nothing of the danger lurking behind those locked doors and boarded windows.

Instead of climbing the rotting steps, Lissa stood on the grass, her face wistful, and gazed at the house. She was still too close, much closer than I dared go. Could she hear anything stirring behind the walls?

"Oh, MacDuff," Lissa said. "Think how grand it must have been once. Can't you see guests arriving for parties, all dressed in fine clothes? They'd pull up right here in horse-drawn carriages. Inside the house, there'd be sparkling crystal chandeliers, dozens of candles, platters of delicious food, a band playing a waltz. Ladies and gentlemen would have danced all night long, twirling round and round till dawn."

Lissa held out her arms and spun, as if dancing to music only she could hear. MacDuff cocked his head and watched.

Georgie snickered, and I grabbed his arm as if I meant to pinch him. "Hush, she'll hear you," I whispered.

After a few seconds, Lissa dropped her arms and curtsied as if she were thanking an invisible partner for the dance. Then, with MacDuff bounding ahead, she walked around the house. Georgie and I followed, as silent as an extra pair of shadows.

At the rear, she climbed the shallow steps leading to the wide brick terrace that ran the length of the house. She sat on a stone bench supported by two crouching lions, their faces streaked with dark stains like tears. It used to be my special seat, my throne. I hadn't even allowed Georgie to sit there.

"She's on your bench," Georgie whispered. "Don't you care?"

I shook my head. Seeing Lissa in my favorite place made me feel closer to her, as if she were truly my friend and I was sharing something important with her.

Georgie sighed and went to work on his mosquito bites. I slapped his hand. "Don't scratch. You'll make them worse."

He pulled away. "I'll scratch if I want to. What does it matter, anyway?"

I shrugged. "Do what you like. I'm sick of arguing with you."

I put some space between us and watched MacDuff run back and forth on the lawn, sniffing and wagging his tail. A pair of mourning doves hunted for food near a shaggy boxwood hedge, cooing to each other in their soft melancholy voices. Somewhere in the woods, a crow called and another answered.

In the fields, insects buzzed and chirped. High in the treetops the wind sighed in the leaves, blowing a few off. They spun through the air and twirled to the ground, landing with a dry rustle.

Lissa sat on the bench, as still as the stone cherubs perched on the terrace steps. She seemed to be watching the clouds, just as I had when I'd sat on that bench.

Georgie shifted his weight and sighed. "She never does anything but moon around. Just like you."

"If you're so bored, go away and do something else. I don't care."

"If I leave, how do I know you won't go over there and start talking to her?"

I stuck out my tongue. "You'll just have to trust me, won't you?"

Georgie made a worse face, but he wasn't sure what to do. Go or stay. Trust me or doubt me. "Promise you won't talk to her," he said at last.

I crossed my fingers behind my back and promised.

"I'll be back soon," he warned me.

In a moment, he was gone, swallowed by the woods as if he were more deer than boy. Left to myself, I continued to watch Lissa. MacDuff had wandered off, and she was alone on the terrace. I wished I knew what she was thinking.

After a while, she walked to the top of the brick steps and looked directly at the tree that hid me.

"I know you're there," she said. "Who are you? What do you want?"

I glanced behind me, thinking Georgie might be hiding nearby to see what I'd do. I heard nothing but a squirrel chattering on a branch and saw nothing but a crow winging from one tree to the next.

"Come out," Lissa shouted. "Let me see your stupid, stealing faces!"

Tense as a deer at the edge of the woods, I stared at Lissa. Did anyone really care if she saw me? Would they even know? Maybe it was time to test the rules.

I drew in my breath as if I were standing on a high dive and took a tentative step toward her, still in the dense shade, still hidden, still safe.

Lissa remained where she was, her eyes fixed on my hiding place. Hands on hips, legs braced, she waited for me to show myself.

MacDuff was at the far end of the lawn, sniffing at something in a pile of old logs, his back to the house, unaware of my presence.

I took another small step. The vines screening me shifted and rustled. Cautiously I stepped into the sunlight and squinted across the ruined lawn at Lissa. Scared as I was, I raised my hand to wave and forced myself to smile.

Instead of returning my smile, Lissa gasped and stepped backward, almost falling over the lion bench. Without taking her eyes off me, she cried, "MacDuff! MacDuff!"

I froze, too shocked to move or speak. Lissa was afraid of me. What was wrong with her? Wasn't I a girl like herself? Why should she be scared?

I longed to run to her and tell her I meant no harm. Surely she'd understand. She must be lonely. Like me, she must want a friend. But I didn't dare approach her now, not with her looking at me as if I were a monster.

Again she called the dog, louder this time, her voice shrill and shaky with fear, her eyes fixed on me.

MacDuff heard Lissa this time. He started to run to her, but when he saw me, he swerved across the field in my direction, barking fiercely. In desperation, I turned and fled into the woods, stumbling over roots and stones, crying as I hadn't cried for years.

Chapter 5

Behind me, I heard Lissa call the dog back. I leaned against a tree, breathing hard. Before I'd caught my breath, Georgie crashed out of the bushes, his face fierce.

"She saw you," he screamed. "You let her see you!"

"Oh, Georgie," I began, but he flung himself at me, pummeling me with his fists. I'd never seen my brother so angry.

"You stepped right out in plain sight," he shouted. "You did it on purpose!"

I shoved him away, grabbed his shoulders, held him at arm's length. "I'm sorry," I cried. "I'm sorry."

He struggled to escape, twisting and flailing like Nero when he didn't want to be held. "Why did you do it, Diana? Why did you break the rules?"

"I told you." I started to cry again. "I wanted to be Lissa's friend, but she was afraid of me. She sicced the dog on me. Why was she scared? What's wrong with me, Georgie?"

"How should I know?" With one huge effort, he broke free of me and ran into the woods.

"Wait!" I called. "I'm sorry, Georgie. Don't be mad."

By the time I caught up with him, Georgie had gotten over the worst of his anger. He got mad quickly and easily, but at least he didn't stay mad long.

"Lissa doesn't know who I am," I told him. "She doesn't know where I live. She's never even seen you. What harm can she do?"

Georgie thought for a while, his forehead creased with concentration. At last he said, "If you stay away from her, maybe she'll think she imagined you. That's what her father will tell her."

I pictured Lissa running home, screaming about something she'd seen in the woods. How would she describe me? I couldn't imagine. But Georgie was right—whatever nonsense she spouted, her father most likely wouldn't believe her. He'd say it was kids playing tricks on her. Maybe he'd tell her to stay away from the old house. Maybe he'd remind her of what the policeman had said about the woods.

Georgie picked up a stick and began drawing little figures in the dirt. "If we stay away from the trailer, maybe nothing bad will happen. Lissa doesn't want to be your friend. Promise not to let her see you again." He dropped the stick and grabbed my wrists so tight it hurt. "Promise"

I mumbled something. At that moment, I had no desire to go near Lissa or the trailer. She'd been scared of me, repulsed. She'd called me a thief, sicced her dog on me. I didn't want to be her friend anymore.

That night, long after Georgie settled down to sleep, I lay beside him, thinking about Lissa. I saw her face again, heard her call the dog to run me off as if I were disgusting, maybe even dangerous. A trespasser. A thief.

What had she seen when she looked at me? What had frightened her? If only I could talk to her—surely I could convince her she was wrong to fear me. But doing that would mean breaking my promise to Georgie. Hadn't I just told him I'd stay away from the trailer?

I looked down at my brother. In the dim light, I saw fear flit across his face as if he were dreaming about the bad thing. "No," he muttered, "no, no. Mother, Mother . . ."

He rolled away from me and curled into a tight little ball, hugging Alfie. I stroked his back gently, soothing him, chasing away the nightmare. "Diana," he murmured, and fell into a deeper, more peaceful sleep.

As quietly as possible, I slid out from under the covers. Nero raised his head, blinked at me, and then cuddled closer to Georgie as if he, too, disapproved of my plans.

Outside, a curl of mist floated above the ground at the edge of the woods. The albino deer, my favorite, stood chest deep in the mist watching me. He let me come within a foot or two of him. Then he turned and ran, his pale body sliding through the shadows like milk.

From across the dark field, the trailer's windows glowed,

beckoning me as if I had no more willpower than a moth drawn to a candle's flame. How I wished I could be inside with Lissa, playing checkers or reading. We'd swap funny stories that made us laugh till our ribs ached. I'd tell her about Stephen and that kiss. She'd tell me about a boy who'd kissed her. It would be like having Jane back—a friend who'd laugh at the same things I laughed at.

The trouble was Lissa didn't want to be my friend. She didn't want to share her secrets with me.

But I knew how to discover them.

I waited in the cold till the lights went out, one by one, and the trailer was dark. Even then, I lingered to make sure everyone, including MacDuff, was asleep. At last, I stepped carefully onto the cinder block and looked in Lissa's window. On the table beside her bed I saw what I'd come for— her diary.

With Georgie's skill, I slid the window open and climbed into Lissa's room. How still she lay. How peacefully she slept. I longed to wake her and tell her I meant no harm, but if she opened her eyes, I had no doubt she'd scream, more terrified of me in the dark than she'd been in the daylight.

I took the diary and tiptoed back to the window. Making almost no noise, I crawled out. Then I ran across the field. After a quick stop to get Mr. Allesandro's flashlight from the tree, I returned to the shed. Georgie still slept quietly, but Nero had gone off into the dark to hunt.

Blocking the flashlight's beam with my hand, I opened the diary and read the first entries. Most of what Lissa had written I already knew or had guessed. Except for the teddy bear. I hadn't realized he was special. I felt a slight pang of guilt, which vanished when I pictured Lissa's array of stuffed animals and dolls. She had so many. And Georgie had none. Surely he should be allowed to keep Alfie.

I turned the page and found the entry I was looking for.

Dear Dee Dee,

Wait till you hear this—it's so scary you might not even believe me. Dad doesn't. He thinks I imagined the whole thing, but it's true, I swear it is—every single word!

I took MacDuff to the old house today. If I'd known what was going to happen, I wouldn't have gone near the place. I walked around it and found an old terrace at the back. It's in ruins like everything else, but I sat on this pretty lion bench and tried to picture how it must have been once, with flowers and shrubbery and green grass stretching downhill to the woods. Soon I felt those kids watching me again, that same old prickle. I ignored them for a while, but I was getting madder and madder. They'd stolen Tedward and my new bike and my favorite book. So I started yelling at them. Thieves, that's what I called them.

The bushes rustled. They were coming. I was kind of scared, but I screwed my face up into a scowl and waited. And then a monster came out of the trees.

49

Oh, Dee Dee, I've never seen anything so horrible in my life. It was filthy and ragged and its hair was tangled with twigs and leaves. It didn't even look human, Dee Dee. I don't know what it was. Bigfoot maybe. But smaller.

It was really and truly hideous. And it was coming straight toward me.

I was so scared I shook all over. Though I never have, I thought I might faint. I could hardly call MacDuff. My voice just dried up. But he came running and he chased the monster away. As soon as it was gone, I called him back because I was afraid he'd get hurt or maybe killed. Who knows what that thing was? Or how many of them might be hiding in the woods?

I ran all the way home and told Dad, but did he believe me? No, of course not. He said someone must be playing a trick on me. A kid dressed up in a weird outfit maybe. I asked him if he'd please call the police to search the farm and catch it, but of course he just laughed. He said if he called the police for every little thing, he would be like the boy who cried wolf. If something really bad happened, the police would think it was another false alarm and not come.

Dad must hate me. How can he expect me to live here now? I'm never going outside again. Dad says fine, I can spend the whole day on my stupid home-school lessons. If only I could go to a real school and meet real kids instead of ogres in the woods.

Oh, Dee Dee—what was that horrible creature? And what did it want? Does it have Tedward and my bike and my book? What will it

take next? What if it's outside right now, watching me through my
window? Why won't Dad at least buy me some curtains?

  I am really, really scared.

  Love, Lissa

  WHO DID NOT IMAGINE THE MONSTER

  I read the entry two or three times, scarcely able to believe what Lissa had written. How could she think such terrible things about me?

  In my mind's eye, I tried to see myself as she had. It wasn't an easy thing to do. I hadn't thought about my appearance for years. When I'd stepped out of the woods, I'd been wearing what I wore now, what I always wore, a blouse and skirt that had once belonged to Miss Lilian. I'd forgotten how they looked—torn by brambles, stained and faded to the color of earth and moss, fluttering in rags and tatters.

  I spread out my hands and examined them. My skin was grimy with dirt, my nails long and ragged. Briar scratches crisscrossed my arms and hands, as well as my legs and feet. My hair hung below my hips in an unwashed mass of tangles, matted with twigs and leaves and mud.

  Till that moment I hadn't cared what I looked like. No one saw me except Georgie. We were used to each other, he and I.

  But Lissa wasn't. Her clothes were clean and fresh.

So were her hands and face. Her hair shone from shampoo.

Burrowing even deeper under my covers, I wept softly. Once I'd been as clean as Lissa. I'd worn nice clothes, too. My hair had been brushed and combed and shiny. I'd had a mother and a father and a home. And friends. But then the bad thing happened and everything changed. It wasn't my fault. Or Georgie's.

I poked my head out of the covers and took a good, long look at my brother. He, too, was a wild child, dirty and ragged, his hair a long mass of tangles. In fact, we looked like feral children, raised in the wilderness by wolves. Romulus and Remus. Mowgli with a sister.

It was enough to make me cry all over again. How had I let this happen to us? Georgie was my little brother. Why hadn't I taken better care of him?

Thoughts raced through my mind, one after another. Finally, I slipped out from under the blankets and found a pencil in Georgie's and my box of useful items.

Stealing glances at Georgie from time to time, I began to write on a blank page in Lissa's diary:

Dear Lissa,

I did not mean to scare you. Please accept my sincere apologies. I am not a monster. I am a twelve-year-old girl. My name is Diana. I am very lonesome. I hope to be your friend, but after today I'm afraid you have the wrong idea about me.

It's true that my brother, Georgie, and I have spied on you and laughed at you and borrowed certain items, but if you knew us, you would understand. At least I hope you would. We lead a strange and lonely life. It is hard for us to keep clean and nice-looking, but I promise that the next time you see me I will look better. You won't be scared of me.

I hope you do not mind that I have read your diary. I am well aware that diaries contain secrets and are not meant to be shared with others, especially strangers (I once kept a diary myself), but I had to know what you thought of me. I promise I will never read it again. Cross my heart and hope to die if I do.

If you wish to meet me, go to the lion bench tomorrow afternoon and wait for me.

Please do not tell your father. No one must know about Georgie and me. We are not allowed to make friends.

> *In hope,*
>
> *Diana*

I read over what I'd written. In sixth grade, Miss Perry had insisted we all learn to compose proper letters in formal language. She would have been impressed with my grammar and spelling, though she might have found fault with my penmanship. Due to lack of practice, it was a little crooked but far neater than Lissa's large, round, loopy handwriting.

I hesitated. The terrace—was it safe to meet Lissa there?

But where else? Not the trailer—her father would see me. Not in the woods—Georgie might see us. It had to be the terrace. As long as Miss Lilian stayed in the parlor, she had no way to watch the terrace.

With the flashlight in one hand and the diary in the other, I stole once more through the woods and across the field to the dark trailer.

I'd planned to return the diary to Lissa's room, but when MacDuff began barking, I tossed it on the picnic table and ran.

The old Willis house loomed ahead, dark and crooked against the starry sky. What I was about to do terrified me, but I could think of no other way to show Lissa I was a girl like herself.

Chapter 6

I sneaked around the side of the house and crawled into a thicket of bushes growing wild by the wall. There, unknown to any of the caretakers, was a small broken window. Back in the days when Miss Lilian and her cats inhabited the floor above, Georgie and I used it to sneak inside. Cautiously I wriggled through and dropped into the cellar.

A breath of cold, dank air met me, the smell of an old musty cellar shut away from sunlight. I shivered and shined the flashlight into the darkness. The basement was full of snakes, but that didn't worry me. Neither did the rustle of mice in the corners. I feared vague sounds—faint footsteps, mournful sighs, low whispers.

Hoping I was truly alone, I made my way around boxes, barrels, piles of newspapers, and broken furniture. I took care to avoid the dark recesses of the cellar and the door to the storeroom, still locked, its key long lost.

I'd never been in the house without Georgie. By the time I reached the rickety stairs leading to the first floor, my skin was clammy and my legs were shaky. Taking a deep breath, I put my foot on the first step, then the second. Slowly I climbed the stairs, stopping every time one creaked. At the top, I eased the door open and stood on the threshold, peering down the dark hall, first toward the kitchen and then toward the front of the house. No sound. No movement. On tiptoe, I edged along the wall, heading for the main staircase.

The air stank of cat pee and mildew. The floors and walls murmured to each other in creaks and groans. Wallpaper hung from the plaster in long, loose strips. Every now and then a current of air lifted them and their dry whispers joined the other sounds.

At last, I stood at the bottom of the once grand flight of stairs that led to the upper floors. I remembered Miss Lilian descending the very same stairs, dressed in gray, one thin hand grasping the rail, her head high, her eyes scornful. Behind her, my mother knelt and swept the carpeted steps with a whisk broom, collecting the dirt in a dustpan and watching me anxiously.

"You, girl, don't play here," Miss Lilian said. "Your mother's working. She can't be bothered with you now."

The vision was so real I almost ran outside, the way I used to. But tonight the staircase was empty. No one was there. Not Miss Lilian. Not Mother.

As fearful as if the old woman still barred my way, I ran up the steps, staying so close to the wall I brushed against the family pictures hanging there, dusty, flyspecked, faded to pale shades of brown.

Miss Lilian's bedroom was at the end of the hall, the biggest and brightest, with a view of fields and woods and the road beyond. I walked toward the closed door, wincing every time a board creaked under my feet. She wasn't in her room, I told myself. She'd died downstairs with her cats as witnesses. If she'd lingered—and I was sure she had—she'd be in the front parlor, behind its closed door. I knew the rules.

But I also knew the exceptions.

Taking a deep breath, I turned the knob slowly and pushed the bedroom door open.

Again I saw Miss Lilian as I remembered her, sitting in her big bed, watching my mother set down the breakfast tray, waiting while she poured the tea, finally spying me in the doorway. "Go away, thief. You're after my jewelry, but you won't get it. Not while there's breath in my body!"

The bed was as empty as the stairs, its sheets frayed by mice. The jewelry had disappeared years ago, but the closets still held Miss Lilian's clothing—skirts, blouses, and dresses long out of style but of fine quality except for moth holes.

I grabbed some clothes and stuffed them into a pillow-case, too scared to think about what would look best. No time to be choosy. Anything was better than the filthy rags I was wearing.

Half expecting Miss Lilian to stop me, I ran to the bathroom. Although the water had been turned off, Miss Lilian's soaps and shampoos, her combs and brushes and towels, lay where she'd left them, dusty and cobwebbed but still usable.

As I dumped toiletries into the pillowcase, a movement caught my eye. Miss Lilian stood a few inches away, watching me. She was wilder and stranger than ever, her hair long and tangled, her clothes in rags. I gasped and stepped backward and so did she, her face twisted in fear. I thrust out my hands to keep her away and she did the same. Close to fainting, I leaned against the wall and stared at my reflection in the bathroom mirror. No wonder Lissa had been scared when I stepped out of the woods.

Lugging the bulging pillowcase, I hurried to the steps. It didn't matter how much noise I made now. I had to get out. The next time, it might really be Miss Lilian I saw.

At the bottom of the stairs, I stole a quick look at the parlor's closed door. Behind it, I heard barely audible movements and a low sigh.

Clutching my bundle, I fled down the hall to the cellar, tripping over newspapers and boxes in my haste. At any moment, I expected Miss Lilian to scream, "Stop, thief! Do you hear me? Stop!"

I shoved the pillowcase through the cellar window and scrambled out after it. Dropping small things as I ran, I fled into the woods. It was almost dawn. The trees were swathed in morning mist and the fallen leaves were damp and slippery underfoot. A rabbit leapt across my path, and I caught a glimpse of the albino deer in the field. His antlered head turned in my direction.

Before I reached the shed, Georgie came rushing to meet me. "Where have you been, Diana? I had a bad dream. And you weren't here."

I hid Miss Lilian's belongings behind my back and tried to edge past him. "I couldn't sleep," I said. "So I went for a walk."

"What's that?" Georgie grabbed at the bundle.

I thrust him away. "Nothing," I lied, "just some stuff from the trailer."

"I thought we were never going there again."

"Just this one last time."

"But what is it?" Georgie lunged at me again. "I want to see!"

This time he caught hold of the bundle and yanked hard. Out fell the brush, the comb, the soap, the shampoo, all rolling away in different directions.

I scurried around, picking everything up. "I can't stand being dirty anymore, that's all."

Georgie backed away from the soap as if it were poison. "I hope you don't expect me to use that junk!"

"It wouldn't hurt you to take a bath."

"Are you joking? I haven't taken a bath for ages, and neither have you."

"Don't you remember how nice clean clothes feel?"

"I like my clothes the way they are." He sniffed his shirt. "They smell like me."

"Maybe you smell bad," I suggested.

"So what if I do?"

"Look at Nero." I pointed to the cat, sitting in a patch of sunlight, carefully licking his paws and rubbing his face. "He washes."

Giving me a sly grin, Georgie licked the back of his hand and rubbed his face with it. "There, that's my bath."

"I'm ashamed of you," I said. "You're absolutely filthy and you don't even care. What would Mother think?"

Georgie's smile vanished. "Don't say that! Don't! Mother's gone, Diana. She doesn't care what happens to us anymore!"

I glared at him, unable to think about what he'd just said. "Stay dirty, see if I care."

Leaving Georgie to sulk, I ran across the field to the pond. Stripping off my clothes, I let them fall to the ground in a filthy heap. If I washed them, they'd fall to pieces. I waded into the pond, shivering as the cool water rose higher on my legs.

By the time I was belly deep, my skin was a mass of goose bumps, but it didn't bother me the way it once would have. Georgie and I had gotten very tough in the years we'd lived on our own. In fact, nothing ever really hurt us. At least not for long.

Taking a deep breath, I sank under the surface and then stood up, wet all over. I began to scrub. And scrub. And scrub.

When my skin glowed pink and clean, I began working on my hair. At first I made no headway against its obstinate mats and tangles. I shampooed and brushed, shampooed and combed until my scalp throbbed. If I'd had a pair of scissors, I'd have cut it all off.

At last, I managed to pull the comb through my hair from roots to ends. Satisfied I'd done all I could, I waded out of the pond and sat in the sun. As soon as my skin was dry, I pulled on a flowered skirt. It settled on my hips and trailed in the grass. Like the skirt, the blouse I'd taken was several sizes too big, but at least both things were clean and neither was torn or stained. Surely Lissa wouldn't be afraid of me now. Why, even without shoes, I felt almost civilized.

My hair was still wet, so I sat and combed it, tugging at the last of the tangles till I was sure no sticks or leaves clung to it.

Suddenly, Georgie stepped out of the woods and stopped, clearly astonished at the sight of me. "Diana," he whispered. "Is that you?"

"Of course it's me, silly." I laughed and tossed my hair. With no tangles to weigh it down, it flew free around my face, as clean and sweet with shampoo as Lissa's.

Georgie came closer and touched my hair. "I forgot it was so light."

"Yours would be the same color, too, if you'd let me wash it."

Georgie backed away fast. "You're not touching me!"

I spread my hands. "Okay, okay. But if you change your mind—"

"No chance of that." Georgie scrutinized me from a safe distance. "Where did you get those clothes?"

I stood up and twirled so the long flowered skirt floated around me. "Isn't it pretty?"

Georgie stared at me, his eyes fearful. "You didn't get that stuff from the trailer," he whispered. "Those are *her* things. Her clothes. Her soap. Her comb. Her brush. You went in her house, didn't you?"

I shrugged. "We've gone in there before."

"Not since she died," Georgie whispered. "What if you disturbed her?" Under the grime, his face looked pale. "Did you see her?" he persisted. "Or hear her?"

"No." I fidgeted with my hair, unable to meet his eyes. Uneasily, I remembered the faint sounds behind the parlor's closed door and the terror I'd felt as I ran through the dark cellar.

Forgetting his fear of a bath, Georgie came closer. "Something scared you. I can tell."

I shook my head. "Mice," I said. "There was nothing there but mice." Near my foot a grasshopper clung to a tall weed, his antennae turned toward me. I nudged the weed and watched him jump away.

"What made you go inside?" Georgie's voice rose. "You never cared about being dirty before."

I looked at him and wrinkled my nose, deliberately insulting him. "You smell bad, you know that? You stink!"

Georgie drew in his breath sharply. "It's because of Lissa. You still want to be her friend, don't you?"

"No," I lied. "I just don't want to be dirty like you!"

"I hate Lissa." Georgie's eyes filled with tears, streaking his cheeks as they ran down his face. "Nothing's been the same since she came. We never used to fight. I hate her, I hate her!"

Instantly sorry, I reached out for him, but he was already running toward the woods. In a moment, he'd vanished and I was alone in the sunny field.

Maybe I should have run after him and apologized, but he'd made me angry talking like that. I'd gone into the house and taken only what I needed, just a few little things. No one had stopped me. Nothing had happened. At least not yet.

So instead of following Georgie, I sat in the sunshine and braided my hair into a long single plait, as thick and heavy as rope, and tied it with string. When I was done, I felt calmer. Georgie would get over his anger. He'd see I hadn't done anything so terrible.

Nero sat nearby, watching me, his tail flicking. I picked him up and burrowed my face in his soft black fur. "Now I'm as clean as you. And I smell good, too."

The cat twisted out of my arms. In a flash he was gone, bounding through the weeds in pursuit of whatever small animal might cross his path. Maybe he preferred my old familiar smell. Well, let him play with Georgie, then. Persnickety old thing—what did I care? Soon I'd have a new friend, a real friend, a girl to talk to and laugh with.

I squinted at the sun. It was past noon. Had Lissa found her diary? Read what I'd written? Did she plan to meet me at the terrace? Would she really and truly be my friend?

I ran across the field and into the woods, eager to see what she was doing. Near the trailer, I heard Mr. Morrison's voice. I dropped to my knees and crawled noiselessly through the underbrush until I was close enough to see and hear. Lissa sat at the picnic table, surrounded by books, her diary among them. Her father sat across from her, drilling her with math problems. MacDuff lay at his feet, dozing peacefully in the sunlight.

"Come on, Liss," Mr. Morrison said patiently. "You're not concentrating."

Lissa frowned at the page in front of her. "I don't care

whether car A or car B gets to Chicago first. It's a boring problem."

Mr. Morrison sighed and pulled a pipe out of his shirt pocket. I watched him light it. The scent of tobacco drifted across the grass and I breathed it in, reminded of my father. He'd often smelled of the same sort of tobacco, aromatic, a little strong, but, unlike cigarette smoke, pleasant.

I wished I could go closer, join Lissa and her father at the picnic table, sit between them as if I were part of a family again. Filled with longing, I wiped tears from my eyes with the back of my hand. Wish all you want, I told myself, it won't happen.

"You'll never finish the problems at this rate," Mr. Morrison said. "And you've still got science, history, and French to go."

Lissa grimaced and bent her head over the paper. Mr. Morrison leaned on his elbows and smoked, gazing at the fields and woods as if they were his own personal estate. For a moment, he looked right at me. I ducked lower, ready to run, but apparently he was too absorbed in his own thoughts to realize I was just a few feet away.

After a while, Mr. Morrison stretched his long skinny arms and stood up. "Can I trust you to sit here and work on those problems while I go inside and write?"

"Sure." Lissa watched him return to the trailer. The moment the door banged shut behind him, she opened her diary. She read what I'd written, I was certain of it, and then looked right at my hiding place.

"You're there, aren't you?" she said. "Diana, that's your name, and you want to be my friend."

I didn't answer. We were too close to the trailer. Her father might step outside for some reason and hear me.

"I must be crazy, but I'll meet you on the terrace," she said. "I'll have MacDuff with me—for protection. You'd better be telling the truth and you'd better be alone. Don't try anything funny, either."

At the sound of his name, MacDuff raised his head hopefully and watched Lissa run inside. In a few seconds she was back with his leash. While she fastened it to his collar, I took off through the woods, planning to get to the terrace before she did.

I made a wide circle around the house, afraid now of the front windows. The plywood covering them was cracked. Perhaps Miss Lilian was peering out from the dark, watching me go by dressed in her clothes, loathing me even more than before.

Cautiously I approached the terrace and climbed its broad steps. No sign of the old woman. No sound. Hoping she didn't know I was near, I perched on the edge of the lion bench. Intensely aware of the silent house behind me, I waited for Lissa.

A breeze ruffled the weeds growing tall on the lawn,

turning brown now, their seed pods emptying into the air. Above, the sky burned a deep pure October blue. The trees had turned red, gold, brown. Their leaves littered the terrace, blown into piles in the corners.

Despite the sun's warmth, I shivered in the house's gloomy shadow. I pictured Miss Lilian creeping about in the dark rooms the way she used to, her mind racing with crazy thoughts, her heart full of hatred for Georgie and me.

A trickle of sweat ran down my spine. "Please come soon, Lissa," I whispered. "Please like me, please be my friend."

Chapter 7

At last, Lissa and MacDuff walked around the side of the house. I didn't move. I didn't speak. I sat on the lion bench, my skirt spread around me, my hands clasped in my lap, my back straight, and waited for them to see me. To be honest, I was scared. I had no idea what I looked like now. No mirrors, no one to ask but Georgie, who couldn't be trusted to give an honest answer. What if Lissa turned and ran at the sight of me?

MacDuff saw me before Lissa did. He tugged at his leash and barked. At that moment, I wanted nothing more than to flee to the safety of the woods, but I swallowed my fear and rose uneasily to my feet, as if I were a hostess greeting a guest.

With some effort, Lissa held MacDuff back. "Diana? Is that you?"

I smiled, pleased she didn't quite recognize me. I hoped I no longer looked like the monster who'd frightened her. "I washed," I said. "I changed my clothes. Like I said I would."

She came closer. When we were face to face, she smiled, and MacDuff sniffed the hand I held out to him. "Good dog," I whispered.

He tilted his head to the side and regarded me in a friendly way. His tail thumped once, a bit hesitantly.

"You look so different," Lissa blurted out. "Yesterday I thought—" She stopped and blushed. "You read my diary, so I guess you know what I thought."

"I didn't mean to scare you." I laughed, and after a second so did she. We were both nervous, edgy, unsure what to say or do.

When Lissa managed to stop laughing, she said, "You looked like a wild girl, a savage."

We laughed again, even harder. "Wait till you see my brother," I said through my giggles. "He won't take a bath, he won't let me wash or comb his hair, he won't even change his clothes."

"Your parents let him get away with that?" Lissa sounded surprised. "Don't they—"

"Oh, no. They—" I cut myself off. I couldn't tell Lissa everything. Maybe I shouldn't even have mentioned Georgie. "They don't care," I finished, but Lissa seemed to have lost interest in my parents.

She reached out to touch my braid. "Your hair is beautiful, so long and thick and blond—almost white."

"It took forever to comb out the tangles." I winced at the memory. "My scalp's still sore."

We sat down on the lion bench together. MacDuff lay down with his chin on Lissa's clean white tennis shoes.

"I don't have any shoes," I told Lissa, suddenly conscious of my bare feet.

She looked surprised. "What do you do in the winter?"

"My feet are really tough." I held up one foot so she could see the sole, as black and hard as if it were made of leather. "I don't need shoes."

Lissa stretched out her feet. "These are new. Maybe I could give you my old ones." She put one foot next to mine. "We're about the same size."

We smiled at each other. That's what friends did—shared with each other. My heart beat a little faster. Maybe Lissa liked me; maybe I could show her my favorite things—the spring that gushed out of a pile of mossy rocks and ferns, the heron's nest in a dead tree in the marsh, the foxes' den, the albino deer.

Just as I was about to suggest a walk, she leaned toward me, the smile gone from her face.

"Did you and your brother steal my bike and the other things?" she asked. "I won't be mad. I just want them back."

Shame heated my face. Maybe Lissa didn't want to be my friend after all. Maybe she just wanted her bike and her book and her teddy bear.

"We didn't steal your bike," I told her. "We borrowed it one night to take a ride, that's all, but Georgie crashed into a tree and wrecked it. We were scared to bring it back, so we hid it down in the woods."

"It was brand-new," Lissa said. "Dad gave it to me for my birthday. He can't afford to buy another one."

"I'm sorry." I twisted my braid, tugging till my sore scalp hurt.

Lissa looked at me without smiling. "What about my book?" she asked. "And my bear?"

"I'm reading *Lassie* to Georgie," I said. "He loves it. Can we keep it a little longer? We're halfway through already."

Lissa considered this. "I've read it five times, so I guess I can wait." She looked at me, squinting in the sunlight. "It's my favorite book."

"It's my favorite book, too. I've read it at least five myself." I smiled at her, happy we had something in common. "It wasn't stealing, you know. We borrowed it, like a library book. We were going to bring it back."

Lissa gave me a half smile and said, "What about my bear?"

I pictured Georgie, sleeping happily with Alfie. How could I take the bear away from him? He'd be heartbroken.

"I know the bear's special to you," I said slowly, "but it's special to Georgie, too. He used to have one just like it, but Miss—" I stopped myself just in time. "You have so many toys. Couldn't Georgie keep it for a while?"

"You don't understand. My mother gave it to me." Lissa's

eyes filled with tears. "She died when I was only five. I can hardly remember her, but when I hold Tedward, it's almost like she's with me again."

I touched her arm, full of sympathy for her and for Georgie as well. "Please, Lissa. Georgie will take good care of your bear."

Lissa folded her arms across her chest and frowned at the woods. I looked at her, wishing I knew what to say or do. Making friends was harder than I remembered. Or maybe I was just out of practice.

"Where's Georgie now?" Lissa asked suddenly.

I shrugged. "He's probably fishing at the pond or holed up in a tree somewhere. Maybe he's catching frogs in the marsh. He often disappears all day."

Lissa looked at me curiously. "You seem to know a lot about the farm. Do you live near here?"

"Yes." I folded my hands in my lap and watched a red leaf spin past my feet. It made a tiny scuttling sound on the terrace. I wished Lissa would stop asking questions. It was tiring.

"In those houses across the highway?"

"Yes." The red leaf settled down in the corner with the other leaves. Two more followed it. Scuttle, scuttle across the terrace, like tiny footsteps.

"Do your parents know you come here after dark?"

I shook my head. "We sneak out."

"You're pretty good at sneaking," Lissa said. "Out of your house. Into my house." She was mad again, I could tell by her voice and the sharp look she gave me.

"I promise I won't borrow anything else," I said. "Unless I ask first."

"How about Georgie?"

"I'll make him promise, too."

"You'd better."

"I'm sorry, honest I am," I told her. "But we've always taken stuff from the caretakers. They were lazy, mean old men, not like you and your father. You're the first girl who's ever come here. Please, Lissa, don't be mad. I haven't had a friend for a long, long time."

Lissa hesitated. "I want my bear," she said in a low voice, close to tears again. "Bring him back and we can be friends."

Before I could answer, we were interrupted by a series of whoops and hollers from the woods. Georgie dashed up the hill toward us, his face and body painted with red and yellow mud from the creek. Crow and hawk feathers jutted from his hair. He wore nothing but a ragged loincloth.

"Go home," he shouted at Lissa, "and don't come near my sister again—or you'll be sorry!"

Lissa gasped and dropped MacDuff's leash. The dog raced across the lawn toward Georgie.

I ran after MacDuff, screaming at Lissa. "Call him off, call him off! That's my brother!"

"MacDuff!" Lissa cried. "MacDuff!"

The dog had already caught Georgie and knocked him down. He stood over him, snarling. While Georgie lay on the ground and hollered, I grabbed MacDuff's leash and tried to pull him away. In a second, Lissa was beside me, yelling at the dog, tugging at his collar.

At last, MacDuff allowed Lissa to haul him away from Georgie. I knelt beside my brother. "Are you all right?"

He sat up, looking more savage than ever. "You liar, I knew you'd sneak off and see her!"

Lissa stared at him, struggling to restrain MacDuff. The dog kept barking. The racket echoed from the house and the woods, setting off a flock of crows.

"Stop it, MacDuff!" Lissa shouted, adding to the din. "Be quiet! Sit!"

Georgie scrambled to his feet. "Shut up and go away!" he yelled at Lissa. "And make that stupid dog be quiet. She's bound to hear the noise he's making!"

"Who?" Lissa looked at Georgie. "Who will hear?"

I grabbed my brother and shook him. "Don't say another word!"

He pulled loose. "I can say whatever I want. Thanks to you, the rules are busted. Nothing matters now."

Lissa turned to me. "What's he talking about?"

I stood between Lissa and Georgie, unsure whose side to take. I was furious with my brother for messing things up just when I was getting to know Lissa, but there he stood, ready to cry, though Lissa wouldn't have guessed it from his fierce expression. Georgie had good reason to be angry. As he'd said, I was a liar. I'd broken promises. I'd broken rules. All because I wanted a friend.

Just as I was about to take Georgie's hand and run, Lissa said, "Here comes my father."

Horrified, I spun around and watched as Mr. Morrison strode toward us. It was one thing for Lissa to know about Georgie and me. She was just a kid like us. But Mr. Morrison was an adult. He was bound to ask even more questions than Lissa. And he'd be harder to fool.

"What's going on?" Mr. Morrison asked, obviously puzzled by Georgie's and my presence. "Who are these children?"

"Diana's my friend and that's her brother, Georgie," Lissa said. "MacDuff tried to bite Georgie. He had him down on the ground. I could hardly pull him off." Lissa started crying. "I was so scared."

Mr. Morrison grabbed the dog's collar and told him to sit and be quiet. MacDuff obeyed, but he watched my brother closely. He'd probably never seen a boy quite like Georgie.

Keeping a grip on MacDuff, Mr. Morrison asked my brother if he was all right. "Did MacDuff bite you? Or hurt you?"

Georgie's thin chest rose and fell sharply with every

quick and angry breath. Ignoring Mr. Morrison, he scowled at me. "You've really done it now, Diana!"

Before I could say a word to stop him, Georgie turned and ran. His skinny legs streaked through the weeds. The feathers in his hair bobbed. He didn't look back, not even when I called his name. In a few seconds, he vanished into the woods. A crow cawed, and then all was still.

I longed to run after my brother, but I stood where I was, too shocked to move. After all these years, I'd let a caretaker catch me. I couldn't believe it. Georgie was right. I'd really done it now.

Mr. Morrison stared at the vines and leaves still swaying from Georgie's plunge into the trees. "I wish he'd let me take a look at him. Are you sure the dog didn't bite him?"

"I'm positive," Lissa answered for me. "He knocked him down, that's all."

"He's okay," I added. "MacDuff just scared him."

Mr. Morrison glanced at MacDuff, who was now lying calmly at his feet. "That's not like you, old boy."

"Maybe it was the feathers in Georgie's hair," Lissa said, "and the war paint. He jumped out of the bushes screaming and yelling. I guess he was trying to frighten us."

Mr. Morrison shook his head. "I've never seen a getup like that. He looked like a genuine savage."

Lissa nodded. "I was scared to death of him."

Her father turned to me. "Well, I'm glad to see you

don't wear feathers in your hair, too." He smiled to show he was teasing, but I didn't trust him. He'd start asking questions any minute now.

Sure enough, his very next words were, "Do you and Georgie live nearby?"

I shrugged and stared at my bare feet, cleaner than they'd been in years, almost unrecognizable. I seemed to have lost my voice as well as the ability to move.

Lissa reached out and took my hand. "Doesn't Diana have the most beautiful hair you ever saw?"

"Why, yes," he said. "With that long braid, you could be a princess in a fairy tale—Rapunzel perhaps."

"Come home with us." Lissa held my hand tighter. "We'll have something cold to drink. Soda, iced tea, lemonade— whatever you want."

Like a creature with no will of my own, I allowed Lissa to lead me back to the trailer. What was done was done. I might as well enjoy having a friend as long as possible.

Chapter 8

Mr. Morrison seated us at the picnic table and went inside to fix lemonade. I told him I wasn't thirsty, but he set a frosty glass down in front of me anyway.

"Where *do* you live, Diana?" he asked again in a friendly way.

"Oh, not very far." I stirred the lemonade with a straw. The ice cubes bumped against each other.

"In that group of houses across the highway from the farm gates?"

I glanced at Lissa and nodded. The ice cubes were miniature icebergs, the kind that sink ships in the Arctic Ocean. *Clinkety, clinkety, clunk.*

"Lissa's bike was stolen the night we moved in," Mr. Morrison went on. "A brand-new blue mountain bike, too expensive to replace, unfortunately. The police thought teenagers from your neighborhood might have taken it. Apparently theft is a problem on the farm."

"I don't know anything about that, sir." I made a special

effort to remember my manners, but I didn't dare look at Lissa. What if she told her father who stole the bike?

"Georgie and I only play here in the daytime," I went on lying, praying Lissa would say nothing. "I know it's private property, but we love the woods."

Mr. Morrison shrugged. "As long as you don't go into the old house, it's fine with me."

Keeping my head down, I ran my finger over the initials Georgie had carved into the tabletop. "I'm not allowed to go in there," I said, telling the truth at last.

"That's good." Mr. Morrison paused to light his pipe. "It's not safe. The floors are in bad shape, and the cellar's full of snakes. Copperheads, someone told me."

"And it's haunted," Lissa put in. "The old lady who used to own it died in the house. I'd love to see her ghost. Wouldn't you?"

Mr. Morrison laughed, but I didn't see anything funny about Lissa's question. If Miss Lilian chose to show herself, I doubted my new friend would enjoy the experience.

"Don't look so solemn, Diana," Mr. Morrison said. "Trust me, there's no ghost in that house. Snakes and spiders and mice. Squirrels. Bats. But no ghost—I guarantee it."

Lissa leaned toward her father. "One of those policemen thought—"

Mr. Morrison shook his head in exasperation. "Oh, for goodness sake, Lissa, only ignorant people believe in ghosts."

Lissa gave him a look I remembered giving my father from time to time. "You don't know everything, Dad."

If I'd dared, I'd have agreed with her. Mr. Morrison definitely didn't know everything. But neither did Lissa.

Mr. Morrison smiled and fidgeted with his pipe, which must be one reason people smoke—it gives them something to do while they think of what to say next.

Changing the subject completely, he turned his attention to me. "Why aren't you and your brother in school today?"

The question took me by surprise. For a moment, I was speechless. "We don't go——" I started to say, and then checked myself. "We're homeschooled. We finished early today."

"Just like me," Lissa said with a smile, not realizing that she herself had given me the idea. Before I'd heard her and Mr. Morrison talking about her lessons, I'd never known of such a thing.

Well, that launched a slew of questions from Mr. Morrison that I could answer only in the vaguest way. But he didn't seem to suspect anything. He smiled and puffed on his pipe, blowing a smoke ring or two to entertain us. We ended up talking about books we loved—*Oliver Twist* and *Treasure Island, Great Expectations* and *Kidnapped, Jane Eyre, Wuthering Heights, The Call of the Wild, The Jungle Books,* and, of course, *Lassie Come-Home.* I was the only one, however, who'd read *Clematis,* so I promised to lend it to Lissa— who'd never even heard of it.

"It must be an old book," Mr. Morrison said. "Probably out of print."

"Yes," I said. "It was written a long time ago, but it's a good story."

At last, Mr. Morrison went inside to work on his own book—a mystery, he said, which he hadn't quite solved.

Lissa and I remained at the picnic table, but MacDuff climbed the steps and pawed at the screen door. Mr. Morrison let him in. A few moments later, the computer keys began their soft *clickety-clack, clickety-clack*.

Lissa looked at me. "You haven't drunk your lemonade."

I pushed the glass away. "I told you I wasn't thirsty. In fact, I don't even like lemonade."

"You should have told Dad. He would've brought you a soda instead."

"I'm really not thirsty," I repeated. I knew I should say something more, but what? I'd forgotten how to put words together in a clever way, to be funny, to be interesting. Worse yet, I had so many secrets. What if I said something that gave me away?

Fortunately Lissa was very talkative. In fact, the less I talked, the more she said. She told me about all the places she'd lived before coming to the old Willis place. Clearwater, Florida, had been her favorite—she'd swum every day and walked on the beach and collected seashells and pretty stones almost as clear as glass.

"Why do you move so much?" I asked her.

Her face suddenly serious, Lissa fidgeted with a splinter of wood jutting up from the table. "After Mom died," she said slowly, "Dad quit his job and sold our house. He takes part-time jobs so he can write. We stay in a place just long enough for me to get used to it, and then he's off again."

Lissa sighed and rested her chin in her hands. "I wish we could live in a nice little house somewhere. I'd love to go to school like other kids. Make friends. Live a normal, ordinary life."

"Me, too." I spoke with more feeling than I'd meant to—or should have.

Lissa raised her head and looked at me sharply. "Why do you say that? You're not stuck on the farm like me. Even if you're homeschooled, you must have friends in your neighborhood."

Instead of answering, I ran my finger around the initials I'd carved long ago on the picnic table. "D.A.E."—Diana Alice Eldridge, right next to Georgie's initials. Being stuck on the farm—my brother and I knew a lot more about that than Lissa did.

"I'm not allowed to be seen with other kids," I told Lissa, rather pleased with the way I'd worded my answer. "I'm breaking the rules just sitting here with you."

Lissa stared at me, clearly shocked. "Your parents don't let you have friends?"

I lowered my head and went back to tracing my initials

on the tabletop. Lissa must have thought I was very strange. A girl whose parents didn't allow her to have friends—how peculiar, how bizarre, how weird.

Before I had time to think of an explanation, Lissa leaned toward me, her face solemn. "Do you belong to one of those weird religions? A cult? Is that why you can't associate with other kids? Or go to public school? Or wear ordinary clothes?"

Even though I wasn't sure what she meant, I nodded. Let her think what she liked about my parents—and their weird religion. As long as it stopped her from asking questions, I didn't care.

"I bet they don't let you watch TV or go to the movies." Lissa leaned across the table, smiling sympathetically. "They probably don't allow you to wear jeans, either. Or drink sugary stuff like lemonade."

"The rules are very strict," I said. "You and I will have to be secret friends—"

Lissa grabbed my hands and squeezed them tight. "Secret friends forever," she whispered solemnly. "Your parents will never see me, never know about me. I promise."

I let my hands stay in hers till she let them go. It was like being with Jane again, holding hands and sharing things. I wished I could tell Lissa everything about me. But I didn't dare begin. How could I explain things *I* didn't understand?

For a while neither of us spoke. That was nice, too, the

quiet between us, disturbed only by birds singing. Overhead, the autumn breeze tugged more leaves from the trees and sent them spiraling slowly down around us, yellow and red, as quick as little fish gathering in pools.

After a while, Lissa smiled at me, cheerful again. "What's your favorite color?"

"Blue, green, red—I don't know. I love them all."

"Mine's purple." She grinned. "How about your favorite food?"

"Mint chocolate chip ice cream." No hesitation this time. My mouth watered at the memory of double-dip cones on hot summer afternoons, sticky and cold and sweet.

"Mine's pizza with double cheese and meatballs." Lissa asked a few more questions. Favorite book—*Lassie Come-Home* for both of us. Favorite candy—Hershey's chocolate almond bars for both of us. Favorite baseball team—the Baltimore Orioles for her and the New York Yankees for me.

Lissa paused to think. "Who's your favorite actor?"

Easy, I thought. "Roy Rogers. Georgie and I have seen just about every movie he's ever made."

Lissa stared at me as if I were crazy. "Roy Rogers isn't a movie star. It's a fast-food place."

"Roy Rogers is so a movie star," I said, puzzled by her ignorance. What kid didn't love Roy Rogers? How could she confuse him with a fast-food place—whatever that was.

"His wife is Dale Evans," I went on. "She's in his movies,

too. He rides a horse named Trigger, a beautiful golden palomino. This funny old guy, Gabby Hayes, is his sidekick. Sometimes he sings cowboy songs. Surely you've seen his movies. . . ."

I stopped, embarrassed by the expression on Lissa's face. "Don't you like Westerns?"

She made a face and shook her head. "They have too much shooting in them. Dad loves Clint Eastwood, though. *The Good, the Bad, and the Ugly, Hang 'Em High, A Fistful of Dollars*. He watches them over and over again. But Clint Eastwood doesn't sing cowboy songs."

It was my turn to stare at Lissa. Who was Clint Eastwood? And just how many years had gone by since Georgie and I had watched Roy Rogers gallop across the desert, chasing cattle rustlers or claim jumpers? More years than I wanted to think about, certainly more than Lissa would believe. Georgie was right. I never should have gotten the two of us into this situation. What had I been thinking?

I looked toward the woods uneasily. It was late afternoon now, and the air had the chilly edge of fall. Georgie was probably hiding somewhere, too mad to go home. I hated for him to be away after dark. The shed was lonely at night.

"I'd better find my brother," I told Lissa, anxious to leave before I said any more dumb things.

"Why was he so mad at you today?" she asked.

"He doesn't want me to be friends with you," I said. "Because—"

"I know, I know," Lissa interrupted. "He's scared your parents will find out and punish you."

I ran my finger around my initials again. If only I were an ordinary girl like Lissa, uncomplicated, with no secrets.

Lissa jumped to her feet. "Let's go find Georgie together," she said. "I want to talk to him."

I looked up, surprised by her sudden interest in my brother. "Why?"

Lissa shrugged. "Maybe if he gets to know me, he'll like me, and then he won't be mad anymore and we can all be friends."

I wished things were as simple as Lissa thought. Reluctantly I led her down a deer trail into the woods, one of Georgie's and my favorite paths. We saw three or four does and the albino stag flash through the trees ahead, sunlight dappling their flanks.

Lissa watched them vanish, delighted for even a glimpse. "It's like magic here," she said, "an enchanted forest where anything can happen."

I looked around, trying to see the familiar woods as Lissa saw them. I'd been here so long I'd gotten used to the trees and the deer, the shadows and sunlight, the slow turn of the years from season to season.

I smiled. Lissa was certainly right about the farm and its woods and fields—anything could happen here.

Chapter 9

A few minutes later, Lissa grabbed my arm and pointed. "There he is—see him? In the field."

At the sound of Lissa's voice, Georgie turned and looked back at us. In his loincloth and war paint, his hair matted with burrs and feathers, he really did look like a wild creature, small and fierce among the towering goldenrod and thistles.

"Georgie," I cried. "Georgie!"

Instead of answering, he ran toward the shelter of the trees.

"Come back!" I shouted. "Don't run off!"

"Traitor!" he screamed over his shoulder. "Liar!"

With Lissa at my heels, I chased Georgie across the field and into the woods. He ducked and dodged under vines and around trees, flashing in and out of sunlight, his war paint blending into the woods like camouflage.

At last, I caught him and pinned him against a tree, holding him fast. "Will you please listen to me?" I shouted. "It's okay to be friends with Lissa. She won't tell anyone about us. She's promised."

"Your parents will never know you broke the rules," Lissa added.

Georgie frowned at me, obviously puzzled. "Our parents? What do they—"

With my back to Lissa, I pressed one finger to my lips, warning him. "It's okay. We can trust her. Honest."

I felt Georgie's body relax a little. His breathing slowly returned to normal. But he was still clearly upset. "Let me go," he grumbled.

I stepped back and dropped my hands to my sides. He and Lissa studied each other silently for several moments, as if neither was sure what to make of the other.

Lissa spoke first, a little hesitantly. "I know you're mad at Diana and me," she said, "but can't we be friends, Georgie?"

He scowled. "I don't need friends. And neither does Diana. We have each other."

"Don't be rude." My fingers ached to pinch him, but I knew that would only make him madder.

He gave me a nasty look and began stripping leaves from a spindly little bush. The feathers in his hair quivered. "If you want to be her friend," he muttered, "go right ahead. Get in trouble. See if I care. But you can't make me be friends with her."

"He's had a bad temper," I told Lissa, "from the very day he was born." I'd heard Mother laugh about Georgie's rages, but I'd never found them particularly amusing. Now I was downright embarrassed. Foolish as it sounded, I'd actually hoped he'd like Lissa.

"She's letting us keep *Lassie* till I finish reading it to you," I told Georgie, thinking he might be pleased.

"I hate that book." He yanked more leaves from the bush. "Give it back to her."

"Georgie—"

He threw a shower of leaves at me. "She can have her ugly bear, too!"

Georgie finally made Lissa mad. "Fine!" she yelled. "Give me my things right now! If you don't, I'll tell my father who stole them."

"See, Diana? I warned you not to trust her!" Georgie cried in triumph. "She's a liar."

Lissa backed away from us, her hand covering her mouth, as if she wanted to unsay what she'd just said. "I didn't mean it. I won't tell Dad. Honest." She began to cry. "Just give me my bear. Please."

"Georgie," I said softly, "Lissa's mother gave her the bear before she died. It's very special to her."

"Big crybaby. I said she can have it, didn't I?" He turned and ran into the woods. "Wait right there. I'll get her stuff."

Lissa and I sat on a fallen tree and listened to Georgie crash off through the underbrush. A breeze sprang up and tugged more leaves from the trees. They pattered down around us like raindrops.

"I'm sorry." Lissa wiped her eyes with the back of her hand. "I was trying so hard to be nice. I thought he'd be nice, too, but when he wasn't, I got mad."

"It's all right." But I wasn't sure it really was. What if something made Lissa mad again? Would she tell her father after all?

But how could I send her away? Lissa was my friend now. It was so nice to sit beside her with the leaves drifting down around us. There had to be a way to make things right between her and my brother.

After a few minutes, Georgie returned, more quietly than he'd left. Nero stalked beside him, his head and tail high, as if he'd chosen sides.

"Oh," Lissa said, "it's Aladdin, the black cat MacDuff chased up the tree. Is he yours?"

"Yes," Georgie said. "And his name is Nero. Not Aladdin." With a scowl, he thrust the bear at Lissa. "Here. Now go away and leave us alone. Diana and I don't need you hanging around all the time."

Lissa cradled the bear in her arms. "He's dirty," she said. "You got him dirty."

Georgie shoved the book at her. "Take boring old *Lassie*, too." He turned to me. "Let's go, Diana."

"I'm walking Lissa home," I said. "You can come with us if you want."

He stared at me in disbelief. "You really are a traitor," he said coldly. "Something terrible is going to happen. Can't you feel it coming? And it will be your fault, Diana. Yours and hers."

"Don't be silly." Even as I tried to stare Georgie down, I remembered those sounds in the front parlor again, the little rustlings and whisperings behind the closed door. Despite myself, I shivered.

Lissa touched my arm. "What's he talking about?"

"Nothing," I said quickly. "He's just trying to scare me, that's all."

"Huh." Georgie strode away and Nero followed him, one as silent as the other.

"It'll be dark soon," I said to Lissa. "Your father will be looking for you."

I walked back to the trailer with her. Although the sun had barely set, light shone from the kitchen window, and I smelled food cooking. Mr. Morrison looked out and saw us. "Glad you're home," he called. "It's suppertime. How about staying and eating with us, Diana?"

"No, thank you. My parents are expecting me." I was grateful for the excuse Lissa had given me. Those strict parents of mine would never allow me to accept dinner invitations.

Before she went inside, Lissa said, "Meet me at the terrace tomorrow. I have lessons till noon, but after that I'm free."

It made me happy that Lissa wanted to see me, but I dreaded going to the terrace again. I'd risked it this afternoon and nothing had happened. But maybe I shouldn't take the chance again. "Why can't we just meet here?" I asked her.

"Oh, come on, Diana." Lissa gave my braid a playful tug. "Your parents will never know you went near the house. I'll see you there at two, okay?"

Without waiting for an answer, she ran up the steps. The door banged shut behind her, and MacDuff barked once, a kind of greeting. Without Lissa, the evening was empty, the dusk damp and cold.

I lingered in the shadows by the window and watched Lissa and her dad move around the kitchen, laughing and talking. I wished I were inside with them, helping set the table, joining in their conversation, sitting down with them in the lamplight. The aroma of tomato sauce drifted outside, rich with oregano and garlic. I breathed in deeply, almost tasting it. Most of the time I was happy not to have to bother with food, but tonight I hungered for a mouthful of pasta, steaming hot, drowned in sauce, dusted with Parmesan.

Sadly I turned my back on the steamy kitchen window and trudged across the field toward the woods. Crickets chirped in the weeds. Every night there were fewer of them. Winter was coming. We'd already had frost. Soon their voices would be silenced. It was a sad time of year.

A fox barked nearby—the vixen, I supposed—warning the kits I was coming. The albino deer leapt into the woods ahead of me, his antlered head high. The does followed, their necks extended, their tails white flags in the darkness.

By the time I reached the shed, Georgie was already asleep, burrowed deep under his blankets, Nero beside him. All I could see of my brother were the feathers stuck in his hair.

I took off my clean clothes and folded them neatly, something I hadn't done for years. I pulled one of Miss Lilian's flannel nightgowns over my head and slid quietly under the covers.

I was tempted to wake Georgie and try to explain about Lissa and me, but I doubted it would help. My brother swung between moods like a man on a trapeze—now up, now down; now here, now there. Whether I apologized or not, he'd get over his anger. He always did.

This time, it might take a little longer than usual. I'd never betrayed him before.

Hours passed. Georgie slept deeply, undisturbed by bad dreams, in no need of comforting. I lay beside him, plagued with worries and doubts. Maybe Lissa was awake, too. I pictured her in bed, reading *Lassie Come-Home,* her little bear tucked in safely beside her, so cozy, so comfortable in her room. She had no idea how fragile everything was. How easily it vanished just when you thought it was yours forever.

I cried then. Cried for my old life, my parents, our warm, snug house. Cried for Georgie, sleeping beside me with feathers in his hair, growing wilder every year.

THE DIARY OF LISSA MORRISON

Dear Dee Dee,

Today I met Diana, the girl who scared me so badly yesterday. And guess what?? She's not a monster after all.

Here's how I found out. She came to my room last night and stole (or, as she says, "borrowed") this diary. She read what I'd written to you about her and it hurt her feelings. Well, that's the risk you take when you snoop into someone else's private thoughts. But it turned out for the best. She cleaned herself up and wrote a note in my diary—would I meet her on the terrace of the old house? I was kind of scared so I took MacDuff, and there she was, waiting on the lion bench like a princess.

Since she's promised never to read another word I write to you, Dee Dee, I will tell you what I think of Diana—and hope she keeps her word and doesn't "borrow" my diary again. She's pretty, but her clothes are strange and old-fashioned, and she has no shoes. Not one pair!!! She says she doesn't need them—not even in the winter—because her feet are tough.

Her hair is so blond it's silvery white, and she wears it in a long, thick braid hanging down below her waist. Dad told her she reminded him of Rapunzel. For once, he's exactly right. Diana's just the sort of girl you might read about in a book written a long time ago—a princess under a spell, maybe. All she needs is a garland of flowers in her hair.

It's as if she's not living in the same world as most people. You have to call her back sometimes, otherwise she'll drift away into the woods and disappear. Do you know what I mean, Dee Dee? It's so hard to put things in words.

It's not just her looks that make her different from anyone I know. It's also the things she says. For example, Roy Rogers is her favorite movie star. All I know about him is the fast-food chain. At dinner, I asked Dad if he ever heard of Roy Rogers the movie star. Dad said he was famous from way back when—not in his time but his parents' time. His mom, my grandmother, had an autographed picture of Roy and Trigger she'd kept since she was a little girl. It wasn't autographed by Roy himself, Dad said, but by someone else, maybe his secretary. Wouldn't that be a fun job—signing movie stars' pictures!

But how would Diana know about those old western movies, I asked. Dad said well, if her parents are as strict as she says, maybe they don't let her and Georgie watch new movies. Maybe they have lots of videos of old Westerns. The kind with no cussing or sex or violence. Just Roy Rogers singing and chasing bad guys wearing black hats.

Dad thinks Diana's sweet and pretty and shy, a very nice girl, but, like me, he doesn't especially care for her brother, Georgie— way too sassy, with those feathers stuck in his hair, and smeared all over with clay like war paint (I'll tell you more about him later).

Dad got on my nerves when he started asking questions about Diana and Georgie's parents. He was so nosy. What do they do for a living? Why do they homeschool their kids? How come they allow them to play on the farm? Don't they worry about them? and so on.

I said I don't know much about Diana's parents, except that they're very strict. I didn't mention the religious cult. He'd probably ask Diana about it, and she'd know I'd talked to him about her.

Now for more about Georgie. He gave me back my book and my bear (poor Tedward—I had to wash him and brush him to make him pretty again), but he was very nasty about it. You'd think I was the one who'd stolen them from him.

My bike is wrecked, though. They hid it in the woods. I doubt I'll ever see it again, which makes me mad. It was a really good bike.

Tomorrow Diana and I are meeting at the old house. She didn't want to because her parents don't allow her to play there. I'm not supposed to go there, either, but I know Dad won't punish me if I do.

Diana says she'd never go in the old house, but that's all I think about. I want to know what it's like inside. Maybe because it's so big and dark and empty. A presence, you could say. Like a haunted house in a story.

As a matter of fact, I'm looking at the old Willis place right now. I can see it from my window. The moon is shining down on it bright as day. I'm sure Miss Willis is in there, roaming around from room to room. Sometimes I think she knows I'm here, and she's waiting for me to pay her a visit. She wants me to come, Dee Dee. I can almost hear her calling me.

Oh, I'm giving myself goose bumps! Maybe Dad's right about my imagination. I'm so silly. What will I dream up next?

If you promise not to tell anyone, Dee Dee, I'll let you in on my secret plan. Dad's going to Home Depot tomorrow to buy stuff to fix the plumbing and maybe some paint, nothing interesting. He loves hardware stores and he always spends hours looking at stuff. He'll be gone a long time. I know where he keeps the key to the house. Guess what I plan to do while Dad's out???

Now I'm going to sleep, dear Dee Dee, and so are you. Good night!

Love, Lissa—

I'll tell you all about the house tomorrow night!

Chapter 10

When I woke, Georgie was gone and so was Nero. I went to the door to see if either was nearby. It was a dull gray day, the sort that tempts you to sleep the morning away. Thick, heavy clouds threatened rain. Leaves blown by a cold autumn wind sailed across the sky, baring trees in the woods. Three deer grazed in the field, a doe and two fawns. Though I made no sound, the mother turned her head toward me. Silently passing a warning to her fawns, she led them into the woods. Of my brother and the cat I saw no sign.

Without Georgie, there was nothing to do but read *Clematis* again. I turned the pages slowly to make the story last, but my thoughts kept straying to my brother. Where was he? Why didn't he come back? He'd been mad at me before, but he'd never stayed away this long.

What if he'd found a place to hide from me? Suppose he refused to forgive me? Suppose he didn't return?

No. That was ridiculous. Georgie couldn't live without me any more than I could live without him. We'd been together too long, bound by secrets we could never share with anyone else. Not even Lissa. Especially not Lissa.

He'd come back soon. At any moment, I'd hear him running through the fallen leaves, calling my name. He wouldn't be mad. He wouldn't care about Lissa. Maybe he'd say he'd changed his mind and we could be friends—all three of us.

But no matter how hard I listened for his footsteps, Georgie didn't appear.

The morning slid past, each hour slower and emptier than the one before. I told myself I wouldn't leave till Georgie came home, I wouldn't meet Lissa, but in the end I couldn't stand the loneliness any longer.

Still hoping to see Georgie somewhere, I followed the path through the woods to Miss Lilian's house. Fallen leaves were ankle deep on the ground. I kicked through them the way I did each fall, watching them fly up in swirls of yellow and red, breathing in their mellow smell.

Sometimes I thought Georgie was following me, spying on me from a hiding place in the woods, but he didn't give himself away. Once or twice I stopped, shivery with goose bumps, and called his name, but he didn't jump out from behind a tree or a bush as I expected. Maybe it was a teenager from the houses across the highway, trying to scare me. That would have been a twist. I didn't dare imagine who else it might be.

At the rear of the old house, I hesitated. Above my head, the trees sighed and murmured. Branches creaked and rubbed against each other.

Without sunlight, the house's pink brick lost its color and faded to an ashy gray. A loose shutter on the second floor banged against the side. The plastic sheeting on the roof rose here and there, tugged by the wind.

The shivery feeling came back, stronger than before. I wished Georgie would step out of the woods and stop me from walking across the field to the terrace. I waited a little longer, giving him a chance to talk me into going home, but he didn't appear.

On the terrace, Lissa waited, dressed for the weather in a thick red sweatshirt and blue jeans. MacDuff loped about on the lawn, following his nose as if he were searching for something. Part of me said, *Go home, hide, don't go near the house,* but a stronger part said, *You've been lonely so long, you deserve a friend.*

If Georgie had been in the shed when I woke up, if I'd met him in the woods, if we'd made up, I might not have left the shelter of the woods. But Lissa was sitting on the lion bench, her head down, looking as lonesome as I felt.

MacDuff saw me before Lissa did. He ran toward me, barking and wagging his tail. I held out my hand for him to sniff and he let me pet him.

"I was afraid you weren't coming." Lissa hugged herself against the wind. "Aren't you cold?"

I glanced down at my skirt and blouse and bare feet and shook my head. I was never really cold, never really hot. Never hungry, never thirsty. But I couldn't very well tell Lissa that without starting another round of questions. I shrugged, as if to say a little wind wouldn't hurt me.

"I can lend you a sweater," she offered. "Or a jacket."

"Thanks, but I'll be okay. I'm used to the cold."

"You are so mysterious, Diana." Lissa looked into my eyes, hungry to learn more about me.

I shrugged again, afraid to tell her anything that might give my secrets away.

Fortunately Lissa never stuck to one subject long. "Where's Georgie today?" she asked.

"He went off somewhere before I got up. He's still mad at me."

"I'm glad I don't have a brother." Lissa sighed. "A sister might be nice, though."

"Oh, Georgie's not so bad."

Lissa raised her eyebrows at that. "Why does he hate me so much?"

"I told you, he doesn't hate you. He's just scared of breaking the rules and being punished."

"What would your parents do to him?" Lissa stared at me. "If they beat him or anything like that, they could be arrested for child abuse."

No matter what I said, Lissa came up with questions I couldn't answer. In an effort to avoid her probing eyes, I looked across the lawn toward the woods, still hoping for a glimpse of Georgie. The wind was blowing harder, whipping the treetops back and forth. Eddies of dead leaves swirled toward us, spiraling up like phantoms from the corners of the terrace.

"A storm's coming," I said. "Maybe we should go to your place. Your dad will be worried."

Lissa pulled the hood of her sweatshirt over her head and drew the drawstring tight under her chin. "Oh, don't worry about Dad. He's at Home Depot, the most boring store in the world. It's jam-packed with tools and plumbing fixtures and nails and screws and I don't know what all. He'll be there for hours."

"But look at the sky." I studied the clouds' dark shapes— flocks of lost sheep straying across a desolate wasteland, blown to rags and tatters by the wind. "It will rain soon."

"Just wait till you see what I have." Lissa reached into the pocket of her jeans and pulled out a rusty key. A small tag hung from it. "I took this from Dad's key ring. Guess what it's for?"

I shrank back, my heart racing like a wild thing. It was a big, old-fashioned house key, maybe one that my father had carried on *his* key ring.

Lissa leaned close to me, her eyes gleaming. "It opens the back door. We can go inside."

On the other side of the brick wall I sensed Miss Lilian

listening, her head up, like a hound on the scent of something.

"I think we should leave," I said. "Now. Before it's too late."

Lissa ignored me. "The old woman who used to live here died in the parlor," she went on. "Dad told me nobody found her body for a week. Isn't that gross?"

"Lissa." I tugged at her arm. "Let's go."

Dropping her voice to a whisper, Lissa pulled me closer. "She never left the house, not even to buy groceries. Her hired man did the shopping for her, but she wouldn't let him in the house. No one was allowed in there. It was filthy, Dad said—cats peeing anywhere they liked, her garbage piled up everywhere, cockroaches, mice, even rats. She was crazy."

"I've heard that." I worked to keep my face blank, my voice expressionless. My own mother had said the same often enough, but she'd never been able to convince my father. Eccentric, he'd argued, but harmless. He should have listened to Mother. She knew Miss Lilian far better than he did.

Lissa waved the key. "You and I could go inside and see the very room she died in. Right now."

"Your father told us not to," I said. "It isn't safe."

"Dad isn't here," Lissa reminded me. "He won't know."

Rain began falling, softly at first, speckling my blouse and skirt with wet spots.

"Come on, Diana." Lissa got to her feet and tugged at my hand. "We'll get drenched out here."

"It's dark inside. You won't be able to see a thing." I didn't want to go into that house again, no matter how hard it rained. Where was Georgie? If he were here, he'd pull me away.

"I already thought of that." Lissa pulled a small flashlight out of her pocket and brandished it.

"We could fall through the floor and end up in the cellar—with the snakes."

"You're afraid!" Lissa laughed. "You think it's haunted, don't you? You're scared of Miss Willis!"

I wanted to cover her mouth to keep her from saying that name. "It's against the rules, Lissa," I blurted out. "I can't go in there! You mustn't go in either! You don't understand—"

"Your parents won't know you broke their silly rules," Lissa cut in.

Before I could stop her, she ran to the door and stuck the key in the lock. With a great deal of effort, she managed to turn it. It made a loud rasping sound. Shoving with her shoulder, she forced the door open. The hinges screeched in protest.

From where I stood, I felt cold dead air rush out to meet me. It smelled of cat pee, garbage, mold, mildew, all the stale odors that had been locked in the house with Miss Lilian.

MacDuff stuck his nose inside. When he caught the whiff of rot and decay, his hackles rose and he whined.

Lissa watched the dog back away from the door. "Mac-Duff," she said, "you silly thing. What's the matter with you?"

Listen to him, I thought, he's smarter than you are. Of course, I didn't say it out loud. No matter how much trouble Lissa caused, I wanted to please her, to keep her as a friend.

MacDuff cocked his head and barked. "Come away, come away," he seemed to say.

Ignoring the dog, Lissa turned to me. "Come on," she urged. "We'll freeze to death out here."

Afraid to let her go by herself, I followed her through the door. MacDuff stayed where he was, but he continued to bark.

With the back door open, the house wasn't as dark as I'd expected. Lissa barely needed the flashlight. But she flicked it on anyway, playing the beam over the ruins of the kitchen. Someone had pulled the stove away from the wall to disconnect the gas line. The top was caked with burned grease, and the oven door hung open. The refrigerator door was gone, its interior stained and streaked. Bottles and jars filled the sink.

I was glad Mother wasn't here to see the state of things. In the old days, the kitchen had been her territory. She'd kept it gleaming and filled with good smells. Where spiders now spun their webs, geraniums had bloomed red and pink on the windowsills.

While I stayed in the doorway, fidgeting and fretting, Lissa explored the kitchen. Undeterred by cobwebs and filth and the rustle of mice burrowing into hiding places, she opened cupboards and investigated rusted cans of food, chipped china, dented pots and pans, empty bottles and jars.

"Look at this," she said loudly. "Miss Willis must have saved every jar of wheat germ she ever bought. I bet there's a hundred of them."

Miss Willis, Miss Willis—the words hung in the still air like a call. "Wake up, Miss Willis, you have visitors."

"Let's go," I begged Lissa, sure I'd heard sounds from deep in the house. "Something's in here. Don't you hear it?"

"Mice," she said, cocking her head to listen. "Squirrels maybe."

I grabbed her arm, but she pulled away, as stubborn as Georgie. "I'm not leaving till I see the rest of the house."

Before I could stop her, Lissa pushed open the kitchen door and ran out into the hall. She stopped at the back stairs, the servants' stairs, the ones my mother used after Mrs. Willis died and Miss Lilian took over.

Lissa pointed the flashlight up into the darkness. "What's that at the top of the steps?"

In the dim light I made out the seat Miss Lilian had installed when she'd gotten too old to climb to the second floor. She sat on it, pushed a button, and it glided up and down the stairs. Before Miss Lilian died, Georgie and I played on it whenever we had a chance, zooming up and down as fast as we could. Miss Lilian would hear the noise and hobble down the hall. If she'd left the seat at the bottom of the stairs, she'd find it at the top. If she'd left it at the top, she'd find it at the bottom.

Georgie and I were too fast for her to catch us in the act, but she knew who was responsible. She'd call our names sometimes. And curse us. We never answered, but she must have heard us laughing. It was such fun to tease the old woman. Didn't she deserve it?

Back then, she couldn't do anything worse to us than she'd already done. But now? I wasn't so sure.

"It's a seat to help handicapped or old people go up and down the stairs," I told Lissa. I was proud of my steady voice, but I hid my shaking hands behind my back.

"Do you think it still works?"

"There's no electricity in the house," I said. "The county turned it off after she died."

Lissa drew in her breath and crossed her arms across her chest as if she were cold. "That seat looks creepy up there. Like it's waiting for Miss Willis."

"The whole place is creepy." I tugged her arm. "Let's go."

Lissa pulled away. "Not yet, Diana. I want to see what's upstairs."

"Those steps will collapse before you're halfway to the top." I tugged her arm again, and again she shook me off.

"There must be another staircase." Lissa pushed past me and headed down the hall toward the front of the house. From an uncovered window high overhead, a little daylight made its way down the curved staircase, illuminating thousands of dust motes dancing in the dim air.

Once more, I saw Miss Lilian sweeping down those stairs, head high, scorning Mother as she passed her, glaring at Georgie and me. How cold her voice, how haughty her manner, how hateful the look on her face. "Go outside, girl. I can't bear the sight of you."

It was rain I heard now, not Miss Lilian's voice. Rain beating against the boarded windows, splashing through holes in the roof, streaking the walls. Rain. And wind creeping through cracks, rattling and banging loose boards and shutters.

But there was something else—little sounds from behind the closed parlor door. Murmurs and sighs, shuffling noises, the tinkle of something small breaking. She was there all right, trapped in that room. As long as no one opened the door, maybe, just maybe . . .

I hesitated, torn between running outside and staying with Lissa, who was already at the top of the steps. "Come on, Diana," she called. I followed her, looking over my shoulder at the parlor door, terrified I'd see it slowly open.

Lissa went straight to Miss Lilian's bedroom, almost as if she'd been guided there. "Look at all this, Diana!" She pointed to the faded velvet drapes hanging at the windows, the cobwebbed chandelier, the fancy marble fireplace, the high-topped walnut bed, the dusty matching furniture.

Yanking open a closet door, Lissa peered inside. "Her clothes are still here." She pawed through Miss Lilian's silk dresses, her velvet gowns, her wool coats, setting them swinging and swaying like ghosts.

While I watched, horrified, she held them up to herself and danced around the room, admiring her reflection in the tarnished mirrors. She tried on hats with plumes, straw hats, knit caps, even a cowboy hat from Miss Lilian's riding days. She wrapped shawls around her shoulders, draped herself with scarves, and struck silly poses like a model in a fashion magazine.

"Here, try this one, Diana." Lissa held up a blue beaded dress, one of Miss Lilian's favorites. The last time she'd worn it, she'd slapped me for spilling a tray of drinks she'd given me to serve the guests.

I pushed the dress aside, hating the dusty feel of the fabric. The smell of Miss Lilian's perfume still clung to it.

Lissa shrugged and grabbed a large straw hat covered with artificial flowers, another of Miss Lilian's favorites. She struck a silly pose. "Isn't this the most hideous hat you ever saw?"

"Please, Lissa," I begged, "put those things away. Your father will see the mess and know someone's been in here."

Reluctantly Lissa began picking up the clothing, but she insisted on wearing the flowered hat. In hope of getting her out of the house, I helped jam dresses and shoes, skirts and blouses, coats and jackets back into the closet. Despite the noise we were making, I heard other sounds from the floor below.

"Listen," I whispered to Lissa. "Do you hear that?"

She stopped chattering, her face solemn for a moment. "What?"

"A sort of rustling and whispering, floors creaking."

Lissa stayed silent, listening hard, and then shook her head. "It's just old house sounds."

After I persuaded her to leave Miss Lilian's room, Lissa looked in the other bedrooms, empty except for odds and ends of broken furniture, mildewed books, and faded pictures, things Miss Lilian had left behind, needed no longer.

"Is this her, do you think?" Lissa held up a framed photograph of Miss Lilian sitting on the lion bench, frowning at the camera, eyes squinted against the sun, a cigarette in one hand and a glass in the other. "She looks like a witch, doesn't she?"

Taken by surprise, I backed away from the picture. How

often had I seen Miss Lilian sitting on that bench, smoking, drinking a glass of wine, her mouth drawn down with disapproval? I even recognized her dress—navy with a prim white collar and cuffs, buttoned tightly. In those days, she'd always dressed for dinner.

"She *was* a witch." I spoke without thinking, but Lissa saw nothing out of the ordinary in my words.

"That's what everyone says." Lissa pitched the photo into the corner. I heard the glass break. "Old witch," she said with a giggle.

"Can we go now?" I started toward the stairs, frightened by Lissa's recklessness. I had to get her out of the house before she did any more damage.

But Lissa was obstinate. Grabbing my arm to stop me from leaving, she shined her flashlight up a dark flight of steps leading to the third floor. "Don't you want to see what's up there?"

"No." I pulled away from her.

"Diana, don't be such a scaredy-cat!" Lissa caught my arm again and tugged me toward the dark staircase. "I might never get another chance to explore this place."

At the top, Lissa drew in her breath at the sight of the grand piano. Without a second's hesitation, she ran to it and lifted the lid. It creaked so loudly I jumped.

"Can you play?" she asked me.

"Don't touch that," I whispered. "Please, Lissa."

"Why not? Who'll hear? Who'll care?" Brushing me aside, she set her flashlight down and struck the yellowed keys. The sound was discordant, warped, tuneless, but she banged away, trying to play "Chopsticks."

"Stop!" In a panic, I grabbed her and yanked her away from Miss Lilian's precious Steinway. "No one's allowed to touch the piano!"

For a moment we struggled. Lissa obviously didn't like being told what to do. Finally, she broke away from me and picked up the hat she'd lost in our tussle. Setting it firmly on her head, she deliberately pounded the piano keys, producing a hideous, tuneless sound.

I wanted to slap her, but as I raised my hand I remembered Miss Lilian's palm striking my cheek, the flash of pain. I shrank back from Lissa, fearful of who I might become, of what I might do. "It's against the rules!"

"The rules, the rules, the stupid rules. Everything's against the rules. How can you have any fun when you're always worried about breaking rules?"

"You don't understand," I said. "If Georgie or I—" I burst into tears, too frightened of Miss Lilian to go on.

Lissa's mood shifted. Abandoning the piano, she gave me a quick hug. "Oh, Diana, I'm sorry. I didn't mean to upset you. I just wanted to explore the house. It's almost as if, as if . . ." She paused and adjusted the hat's angle.

"As if what?" There was something she wasn't telling me,

something that worried me. I shivered, intensely aware of the darkness around us.

Lissa tilted the hat over one eye and then shifted it the other way. Nervous. Unsure. "I don't know," she said slowly. "I just had to see the house. I *had* to."

Over our heads, thunder rumbled. The heavy drapes swayed as the wind found its way through the boards covering the windows. Downstairs something thumped softly. I heard it again and then again, a little louder each time.

"Please, Lissa," I begged. "Let's go. Before it's too late."

She stared at me. "Too late for what?"

"Your father," I blurted, thinking fast. "He'll come home and you won't be there and he'll start looking for you. If he finds us in here . . ." I let my words trail away, unsure what to say next. "Well, you'll be in trouble for sure. And so will I."

Lissa shrugged. "Dad isn't strict like your parents. We'll just have a little talk and that'll be that." She shined the flashlight around the room again, letting its light play on old paintings, books, an ornate carved marble fireplace. "I guess I've seen just about everything up here," she said at last.

Aiming the light in front of us, Lissa followed me downstairs. On the second floor, she paused and looked at Miss Lilian's bedroom. "Are you sure you've never seen her ghost?" she asked.

My mouth was too dry to answer, so I simply shook my head and tugged her sleeve, urging her not to linger.

Suddenly, Lissa rushed past me, her feet thudding on the stairs. She bumped the old photographs hanging crooked on the walls, brushed the strips of torn paper aside, and came to a stop at the bottom.

Turning to me, she said, "Dare me to open the parlor door?"

Chapter 11

I ran down the steps after Lissa. In a panic, I jerked her hand away from the knob. "Don't open that door!"

"I want to see where she died." Lissa reached for the knob again. Miss Lilian's hat hid her face, but her voice was shrill with excitement. The rustling sounds grew louder, as if someone in a silk dress was crossing the room. The floor creaked, and the air turned so cold my teeth chattered.

As clearly as if she was standing beside me, I heard Miss Lilian's voice in my ear. "Get out of the girl's way, Diana. Let her open the door."

Instead of obeying the old woman, I pressed my back against the door and pushed Lissa away with all my strength. She staggered backward and crashed against the wall.

"What's wrong with you?" Lissa rubbed her arm and winced as if I'd hurt her. "Are you nuts?"

"Just stay away from the door. If you open it, she'll get out!"

"What are you talking about? Who'll get out?"

In my ear, Miss Lilian's cold voice froze the very air between us. "Let the girl open the door. You and I have business to settle, miss."

"Please, Lissa, please!" I flung myself at her. "I beg you, we have to get out of here."

But Lissa evaded me and reached for the knob. "I have to open the door," she cried. "I have to!"

"That's right," Miss Lilian hissed, "she must open the door. She must, she must."

Despite my efforts, Lissa managed to turn the knob. The door swung open and slammed against the wall with a loud bang. Out poured a blast of cold air. It spun past us like a small cyclone of ice, taking the flowered hat with it, and whirled up the stairs, leaving us frozen speechless in the parlor doorway.

Suddenly, there she was, Miss Lilian herself, peering down at Lissa and me from the top of the stairs. She was just as I remembered—tall and gaunt, bent with arthritis, wrathful, hateful. Uncombed hair framed her pale face in thorny white brambles. Clutching her hat, she leaned over the railing and directed her gaze at me. "You! You!"

She stood there, her mouth moving as if she wanted to say more but could find no words. "You," she whispered. "You and your brother. Just wait!"

With a wail of fury, she turned and fled. Her gray silk

dress rustled. Her footsteps clicked the way they always had. Then her bedroom door slammed shut, and she was gone.

In the sudden silence, I collapsed on the steps, weak with fear. Miss Lilian was free. Free to pursue Georgie and me, free to hurt us again and again. With her hunting us, we weren't safe anywhere on the farm. And we couldn't leave.

I glanced at Lissa. What had she done? I wanted to scream at her, to blame everything on her, but she sagged against the wall as if she'd never move again, her face color-less, her eyes unfocused. While I watched, she drew in her breath, opened her mouth, and began to scream.

Out of pity, I took Lissa's hand and pulled her to her feet. I ran and dragged her behind me, still screaming, stumbling and tripping and bumping into things as if she were blind.

"Faster!" I yelled, jerking her along. I didn't care if I was hurting her, I didn't care if I was scaring her. It was her fault. She'd brought me here, she'd insisted on seeing every room in the house, she'd opened the parlor door.

At last, we plunged outside into cold, fresh air smelling of nothing but rain. MacDuff leapt up from the terrace and bounded ahead across the weedy lawn, as anxious as we were to get away from the house.

Once safe in the trailer, we slammed the door against the wind and rain and whatever else might be out there. Without speaking, we huddled on the sofa, wet and cold and shaking. MacDuff cowered between us, as scared as we were. Mr. Morrison wasn't back from Home Depot—which was a good thing, considering Lissa's hysterical weeping.

"Oh, Diana," she cried, "I saw her, I saw Miss Willis! She ran up the stairs, she, she—" Lissa's sobs overcame her and she buried her face in MacDuff's fur.

"Why didn't you listen to me?" I tried hard not to shout at her, but my voice rose anyway. "I told you not to go in the house, I told you not to open that door!"

Lissa rocked back and forth, crying and moaning. "I couldn't help it, my hand just went to the doorknob. I couldn't stop myself. And she got out. She—"

"She didn't just *get* out. You *let* her out!"

"But I didn't mean to. I told you. It was like my hand, my hand—" Lissa raised her head from MacDuff's back and looked at her hand as if it didn't belong to her. "She made me do it, Diana."

I stared at her. Maybe it was true. Ghosts sometimes possessed people. I'd seen it happen in movies, so maybe it happened in real life, too. "If you'd just listened to me—"

Lissa started crying again. "It wasn't my fault."

I slumped down on the sofa and stared at the window, sheeted with rain. MacDuff whimpered and licked my hand, and I stroked his head. Though I didn't like to admit it, I'd started all this by making friends with Lissa. It wasn't her fault. It was mine. I had no right to be angry with her.

Lissa leaned closer to me, her voice hoarse from crying, and whispered, "What will Miss Willis do? Will she hurt us?"

I kept looking at that window, fearful of seeing a face press itself against the glass. I saw nothing but rain. Where was Miss Lilian? What was she doing all alone in her ruined house? When would she come looking for my brother and me?

"If she comes after anyone," I said slowly, "it will be Georgie and me, not you. It's us she hates."

Lissa huddled in her corner of the sofa and stared at me, her face wet with tears. "Why would she hate you and Georgie?"

I looked at Lissa long and hard, tired of her questions, tired of her ignorance. Why had I wanted a friend so badly? I got to my feet. "I have to find Georgie."

"Don't go." Lissa grabbed my hand with both of hers. "Wait till Daddy comes home. Don't leave me here alone."

"I told you, Miss Willis won't hurt you."

"Please, please!" Lissa clung to me and wept. "Stay with me. I'm scared."

I pulled away from her. "You have MacDuff. But Georgie's out there in the woods with no one but Nero."

"Don't be mad," Lissa begged. "I'm sorry, Diana, I'm so sorry. I didn't know— I didn't mean— I—"

I left her weeping on the couch, her arms around the dog. All I cared about was Georgie. I was his big sister. I had to keep him safe from Miss Lilian.

THE DIARY OF LISSA MORRISON

Dear Dee Dee,

What happened today is almost too terrible to write about. My hand is still shaking so much I can hardly hold my pen. I did what I said I was going to do. I made Diana go inside the house with me. MacDuff wouldn't come with us. Diana didn't want to go in either—she said it was against the rules.

Oh, Dee Dee, I should have listened to Diana. She and MacDuff are both smarter than I am. What's wrong with me? Why do I do dumb things?

As soon as I stepped inside that house, I smelled a horrible stink—cat pee mostly, just disgusting—but did that stop me? Oh, no, I went in anyway. I just had to see what the house was like.

But it was more than that, Dee Dee. It was like something was making me go inside. It was kind of like a voice in my head saying, "Come in, come in." It wasn't just an invitation, Dee Dee, it was more like an order, and I had to do what it said. Hearing voices— it sounds crazy, but that's what it was like.

I hope nobody ever reads what I just wrote. They'd lock me up in a padded cell for sure. But it's true. There was a voice, and now I know it was Miss Willis. She wanted me to come in, she wanted me to open that door.

I was scared, but I didn't want Diana to know, so I said let's go upstairs. We went to Miss Willis's bedroom and I tried on her clothes and made fun of them. I even took one of her hats, a big one with flowers on it, really hideous, and then I made Diana go to the third floor. There was a big old piano up there, all covered with cobwebs. Diana freaked out when I started playing it. We actually had a fight, and then she started crying and I realized I was acting like a spoiled brat, making her do what I wanted when she was so totally worried about those rules—which turned out to be much more important than I ever dreamed.

So I told her I was sorry and we started to leave, but at the bottom of the steps the voice in my head started up again. There I was, right in front of the parlor door, and I knew that was the room where she died, and the voice kept telling me to open the door.

So I grabbed the knob. Diana tried to stop me, but it was like something had ahold of me and it was making me turn the knob and open the door. Honest. I'm not just making excuses for what I did. It was her. Miss Willis. I'm sure of it now.

As soon as the door opened, this icy cold wind came rushing out and I saw something gray go running up the steps. It took the hat, snatched it right off my head, and stopped at the top. Dee Dee, don't think I'm nuts when I tell you this—it was Miss Willis. She looked real, but I knew she was a ghost because she died at least ten years ago. There she was, staring down at Diana and me, mean and ugly with wild white hair, wearing a gray dress like any old crazy woman you might see in a store or walking down the street.

She leaned over the rail and started yelling at Diana. Then she ran down the hall and I heard her bedroom door slam and the house got very, very quiet—as if it was holding its breath till the next thing happened.

That's when I started screaming. I couldn't stop. Maybe I was hysterical. Or losing my mind. Diana grabbed me and yanked me along behind her. She kept saying I had to go faster, but my legs wouldn't work right and I couldn't see, maybe my eyes were shut, I don't know, but I was so scared. We got outside and ran all the way home and MacDuff ran with us. I thought Miss Willis was chasing us, I thought she'd come to the trailer, I thought she'd hurt Diana and me.

Diana says Miss Willis's ghost won't hurt me, she'll go after her and Georgie because she hates them. Not me. But, Dee Dee, what could they have done to Miss Willis? She's been dead so long and Diana's only twelve like me. It's all so strange—her parents, the rules, all the things I don't know about Diana's life. My head hurts when I think about it.

But, no matter what Diana says, I'm still scared and Dad is still at Home Depot, and when he comes home he won't believe a word I say, he'll just be mad because I went into the house when he told me not to. Maybe Dad will find another job soon. I hope so. Far away from here. I see now why all those other caretakers left. I don't know how I'll get a single night's sleep as long as we live here.

Let me tell you something, Dee Dee: never say you want to see a ghost. You will definitely be sorry.

Love, Lissa

Chapter 12

Georgie stood in the shed's doorway, a scowl on his face, watching me run through the rain toward him. He'd applied a fresh coat of war paint and added more feathers to his hair. I supposed that meant he was still mad at me. Well, soon he'd be even madder.

"Were you playing with Lissa again?" he asked, daring me to lie.

Instead of answering, I seized his hands. "Oh, Georgie, Georgie—"

"What's wrong?" he asked, suddenly fearful.

"She's loose! Miss Lilian—I saw her. She's just the same, mean, angry. She said—"

Georgie cut in before I could finish. "How did she get out?" His voice shook and he gripped my hands tightly.

"It was Lissa," I said, too ashamed to meet my brother's eyes. "She took a key, she opened the back door, and I went in with her. I knew I shouldn't, but I was scared to let her go by herself. She went all over the house, she even played the piano, and then she wanted to see where Miss Lilian died, so she——"

"You let her open the parlor door?" Georgie stared at me, white-faced with disbelief and fear.

"I tried to drag her away, but she, she—— Georgie, I couldn't stop her. She was too strong. She says Miss Willis made her do it, she——"

Georgie flung himself at me, terrified. "I told you something horrible would happen. I told you and told you and told you!"

"It's all my fault," I admitted. "I broke the rules. I'm sorry, Georgie, I'm so sorry."

We clung to each other, shivering and shaking, imagining every sound in the woods was Miss Lilian hunting for us. But all we heard were ordinary noises. Wind in the trees, rain pattering on the shed's roof, a fox barking.

At last, Georgie drew back and looked up at me. His war paint was smeared and his feathers were crooked. "Where is she now, Diana?"

"Miss Lilian? In her bedroom. She didn't need that chair to go upstairs, Georgie. She ran up there all by herself."

"Does that mean she can chase us?" My brother's eyes roved to the shed's doorway and the dreary night darkening the field beyond. A damp breeze, carrying the smell of rain and fall's decay, made him shudder. "Can she come here and, and——"

"Maybe she can't leave the house," I whispered. "She must have rules, the same as us." I squeezed his hand, but I didn't tell him what I was thinking. I'd broken the rules. Miss Lilian could break them, too.

Silently I crawled under the blankets beside Georgie. This close, my brother smelled like a little animal, a rabbit perhaps, that lived under bushes in fear of hawks.

"Suppose Miss Lilian can go outside like you and me," Georgie whispered. "What if she comes to the shed while we're asleep? What if she—"

"I won't let her hurt you." I held him so close the feathers in his hair tickled my nose. "I'm your big sister. I'll take care of you."

Georgie relaxed, more trusting than I'd expected, considering I hadn't been the best caretaker lately. Nero crept under the covers and curled up between us, soft and warm. His purr comforted us.

Just when I thought he'd fallen asleep, Georgie rose up slightly and looked into my eyes. "Tell me the story, Diana, all the way to the end."

"But it always scares you."

"Not this time, I promise. I need to remember everything so she can't catch me again."

While Georgie lay still and quiet beside me, I told him the familiar story of our days at Oak Hill Manor with Mother and Daddy. This time when I came to the part where Miss Lilian turned against Georgie and me, he tensed, but he didn't make me stop.

"One day," I whispered, "you cut your leg climbing over a rusty barbed-wire fence. You were bleeding, so I took you to the house to find Mother. She wasn't there, but Miss Lilian caught us in the kitchen and began to rant and rave in her crazy way. We tried to run outside, but she got between us and the kitchen door, so we ran down the cellar stairs to hide."

Georgie nudged me. "Why didn't we run out the front door?"

"We were going to hide in our secret place. Remember?" I stroked his back, soothing him as if he were Nero.

We'd found the little room one afternoon when we were exploring the cellar, way back when we'd first come to Oak Hill Manor. The door was hidden in a dark corner, behind piles of boxes and old furniture. The room itself had no windows and its walls were thick.

Georgie and I had fixed it up like a clubhouse, with candles and books and a few board games, along with blankets and pillows borrowed from the attic. It was a great place to play without fear of being caught by Miss Willis.

"But Miss Lilian came down the steps behind us," Georgie went on for me. "She was waving a broom and screaming at us. We ran into the room and slammed the door. It was a stupid thing to do."

"We thought we were safe," I said. "But she bolted the door and locked us in." In my head, I heard Miss Willis again, just as I heard her in my worst nightmares. "Stay there! Think about how you've treated me. I'll come back when you're ready to apologize."

"And then she left," Georgie whispered. "And she never came back."

"No, she never came back." My heart beat faster. I wished Georgie would say, "Stop," but he lay beside me, still and tense, a rabbit poised for flight. So I went on to the worst part.

"We cried and shouted for Mother and Daddy, we pounded on the door till our fists ached, but no one heard us. No one came. No one let us out."

Georgie shivered and curled into my arms. I could feel his heart beating as fast as mine.

"We lit candles," I told him. "We ate the crackers we'd left there. But after a while the candles burned down and went out. It was so dark. And cold. We told each other stories, we sang songs . . ." I paused, unable to go on.

"What happened next?" Georgie whispered. "Do you remember?"

"I think we fell asleep. At least that's how it seems. A deep sleep."

"And then we woke up," Georgie said, sounding cheerful again, "and we were outside and the sun was shining."

"Yes." After the darkness of the cellar, the light had hurt our eyes, almost blinded us. We stood in a field overgrown with thistles and pokeweed, wild daisies and Queen Anne's lace, swarming with bees and butterflies. At first I'd thought we must be in heaven, but when I looked around, I realized we were still on the farm. The familiar woods lay ahead, their leaves swaying in a summer breeze. The sky was blue, almost cloudless, and a mockingbird sang from a fence post. Grasshoppers jumped around our feet, bees buzzed, a crow cawed in the woods. A tractor rumbled in the distance. The air smelled of honeysuckle and damp grass.

Behind us was Miss Lilian's house, barely visible through a screen of trees in full leaf.

Everything had been just as it should be, yet I'd felt strange. Not thirsty, not hungry, not weak from our days in the dark cellar. It was as if I'd become very light. A gust of wind might send me spinning higher and higher until the earth was a tiny ball lost among stars.

In the dark shed, I squeezed Georgie's hand, glad to feel its warmth. He propped himself up on his elbows, more himself now that the worst part of the story was over, and peered into my eyes.

"How did we get into that field, Diana? Who opened the door? Who let us out?"

"It was like a dream," I said, at a loss for an explanation. "First we were in the cellar, and then we were in the field with nothing in between. *Bing*—there we were in the sunshine."

"We wanted Mother and Daddy," Georgie said, sad now. "We wanted to go home."

"But we couldn't," I said. "It was against the rules."

"The rules," Georgie muttered. "Always the rules. Where did they come from, Diana? Who gave them to us? Do you remember?"

"It wasn't Mother or Daddy," I said.

"They gave us plenty of rules before the bad thing happened." Georgie yawned. "Like not going into Miss Lilian's house and not touching the piano and not talking with our mouths full and not interrupting. And not, and not . . ."

Georgie's voice trailed off into a mumble and he fell asleep, but I lay beside him, thinking, trying to remember. No one had told us the rules, I was sure of that. No one had written them down and handed them to us. They were just there, in our heads:

Rule One: Do not let anyone see you.
Rule Two: Do not leave Oak Hill Manor.

As long as we obeyed those two rules, we could do anything we liked. Play all day, stay up as late as we wanted, roam the woods and fields, tease and play tricks on the living.

The first night of our new life, Georgie and I had crawled through the open kitchen window of our house and crept to our parents' bedroom. The light was out, but they weren't asleep.

"If Miss Lilian recovers," Mother was saying, "she might be able to tell the police something about Diana and Georgie. Maybe she saw something, heard something, maybe——" She broke off and began to cry.

"What could she tell the police?" Daddy asked. "She's been in the hospital since the children disappeared. Out of her head. Irrational. She couldn't possibly know anything about Georgie and Diana."

Georgie and I hid in the shadows, yearning to tell our parents where we were and what had happened, but in those days, the rules held us fast. We dared not speak to Mother and Daddy.

Long after the police and their dogs had given up the search for us, Mother and Daddy kept looking. We followed them through the woods, around the pond, along the creek, to every place we used to go. I think they expected us to pop out from behind a tree, laughing at the prank we'd played on them. At night, we listened to them weep for us, their lost children. We cried, too.

If only we'd told Mother and Daddy about our secret room. They would have found the door and opened it. They would've let us out and the bad thing wouldn't have happened.

Weeks passed. Summer faded into fall. Miss Lilian came home from the hospital, leaning on a cane, a nurse by her side. In no time, she ran the nurse off. She said she didn't need anyone looking after her. Waste of money, she complained to Mother.

Although the police never questioned Miss Lilian, Mother asked her if she remembered anything about the day Georgie and I disappeared. They were sitting on the terrace, Miss Lilian in a lawn chair and Mother on the lion bench, shelling peas into a bowl. Georgie and I hid in the boxwood, close enough to hear every word.

"I had a stroke," Miss Lilian said, as if that were far more important than Georgie's and my disappearance. "I don't know anything about that girl and boy. Don't ask me again!"

"But you must have heard something," Mother persisted. "A car, perhaps; a stranger's voice, a cry—"

With some effort, Miss Lilian got to her feet. "I know nothing about it! Nothing! I almost died myself that day. Or have you forgotten?"

Leaving Mother on the lion bench, Miss Lilian hobbled into the kitchen, thumping her cane with every step.

Mother sat and wept quietly. Although we were near enough to reach out and touch her, we could do nothing but watch. The rules were strict. And harsh.

After a while Miss Lilian came to the door. She stood there a moment, glowering at Mother. "I can't afford to keep you and your husband here any longer," she said. "I want you out of the tenant house in forty-eight hours."

Mother stared at the old woman in disbelief. "But Miss Lilian, who will take care of you?"

"I don't need anyone! Especially you, wasting my time and money moping around, crying, thinking of no one but yourself."

We followed Mother back to the tenant house. Daddy was drinking a cup of coffee in the kitchen.

"Miss Lilian has dismissed us," she told him. "We have two days to pack up and leave the farm."

Daddy sighed and set his cup down. "It's for the best, Alice. We can't stay here. It's too hard."

Mother sat down at the table with him. "But what if they come home and we're not here?"

Daddy shook his head, his face sorrowful. "Don't talk that way," he murmured. "They won't return. You know it and I know it. They're gone."

Mother shook her head. "They're here on the farm. I feel them near me. So close, so . . ." Her voice broke and she began to cry. "How can I leave them?"

Daddy reached for her hands and held them tightly. "They'll always be with us. As long as we live, wherever we go."

And so two days later, Georgie and I hid in the woods and watched Mother and Daddy load their belongings, and ours, into a rental truck. Mother looked tired and sad. Daddy had no smiles, no jokes. He moved slowly, struggling with the weight of mattresses and furniture.

After Daddy loaded the last box, they got into the truck and drove down the lane. Georgie and I followed them through the woods, silently begging them to turn back, to stay near us as we'd stayed near them.

The truck stopped at the gate and Mother stepped out to open it. An autumn breeze stirred her hair and sent a scurry of leaves racing toward her. She looked back at the farm. Softly she called our names, as if she hoped we might finally hear and come running.

Georgie made a move toward her, but I seized his shirt and held him back. "No," I whispered. "We can't go to her. You know that."

He struggled for a moment and then went limp in my arms, his body shaking with sobs, his face against my chest. The rules kept us where we were, as much a part of the farm now as the trees, more firmly rooted to its earth than the deer and foxes.

Silently we watched Daddy drive the truck through the gate. Mother closed it behind him. She lingered, her eyes searching the woods, whispering our names again. Daddy called to her softly, and she climbed into the passenger seat.

The door closed almost noiselessly, and Daddy turned off the engine. They sat together for a long time, talking.

"Maybe they'll change their minds," Georgie whispered. "Maybe they'll stay."

I shook my head. Miss Lilian had fired them. The old stone tenant house was no longer their home.

Finally, Daddy started the truck and turned east on the state road, just two lanes in those days. Georgie and I climbed onto the gate and watched until the truck vanished from sight and the road was empty.

For weeks afterward, Georgie went to the fence and watched for the truck to come back. I didn't go with him. I knew it would never return.

Finally, Georgie got mad and stopped going to the gate. He said Mother and Daddy had forgotten about us, but he was wrong. No one forgets the people they love. I just wished I knew where they'd gone and what had become of them.

Not long after our parents left, Miss Lilian hired a caretaker, a lazy old man named Jimmy Watts. He spent most of his time drinking whiskey and never fixed anything. He did Miss Lilian's grocery shopping, and that was all.

He lasted maybe a year. Then he quit, and Miss Lilian hired Earl Powers. He stole money, jewelry, anything he thought might be valuable. Miss Lilian fired him.

After that, Georgie and I couldn't keep up with the hired men. They came and went, each one as lazy as the one before. None of them bothered with repairs. Paint peeled, ceilings sagged, the roof leaked.

Years passed. Georgie and I lost count of them. We stayed the ages we'd been when the bad thing happened.

But Miss Lilian got older—and crazier. We helped the process when we could. We flitted through rooms, just out of sight, knocking pictures off walls, throwing things, slamming doors, turning lights on and off. We played the Steinway in the middle of the night, filling the darkness with half-remembered music, alarming the cats and terrifying the hired men. Poltergeists, said one. Ghosts, said another.

"I know who you are!" Miss Lilian would yell and brandish her cane. "Leave me alone! You'll be sorry for this!"

Georgie and I laughed. The old woman couldn't scare us now. We hated her and she hated us.

Then things changed again.

One winter day we ran through the house as usual, chasing each other up and down the steps, laughing and shouting, daring Miss Lilian to come after us with her broom. For once she didn't respond to our taunts. No shouts, no curses, no threats, no tottering footsteps.

Georgie and I dashed from hiding place to hiding place, searching for the old woman. Cats meowed and darted out of our way. A starling trapped in the house flew up the stairs to the second floor. We heard its wings flutter as it brushed past us.

The door to the front parlor was closed. Behind it, I sensed an odd silence. An emptiness beyond emptiness. Georgie looked at me, suddenly fearful. I slowly opened the door and peered into the darkness. Miss Lilian sat in her chair by the window, its velvet drapes drawn against the daylight. Still, she sat so still. Too still.

"Is she asleep?" Georgie whispered.

"No," I said. "She's dead."

Georgie and I backed away. With shaking hands, I shut the door as soundlessly as possible. We ran out of the house, leaving her to be found by the hired man.

As we raced home to the shed, new rules established themselves in our heads, just as the old ones had:

Rule Three: Stay away from the house.
Rule Four: Do not disturb Miss Lilian's slumber.

A week or so later, a hearse came for Miss Lilian. It was a cold, rainy day, as dreary as you can imagine. The lane was muddy, the weeds were dry and brown, the trees bare. A flock of crows watched from the oak tree, perched on the branches like mourners in a church.

As the undertakers prepared to leave, one said to the other, "Well, that's that. Almost a hundred years old and not a soul to mourn her."

His companion nodded. "It's a sad thing to die alone."

With that, they slammed the hearse doors and drove away, taking Miss Lilian's body with them.

But not her spirit. Miss Lilian remained in the parlor, just as Georgie and I remained on the farm.

Now, thanks to me, the old woman was free. And I was afraid as I'd never been before.

THE DIARY OF LISSA MORRISON

Dear Dee Dee,

I haven't written to you for a couple of days, but that's because Dad enrolled me in a gymnastics class and I've been busy.

I met a girl named Chelsea who told me about something scary that happened at Oak Hill fifty or sixty years ago. Two children disappeared from the farm, a boy and a girl. The police searched everywhere, but they were never found. To this day no one knows what happened to them.

Chelsea says their ghosts are still here, along with Miss Willis's ghost. Sometimes teenagers come to the farm late at night. She knows several, including her own brother, who say they've seen Miss Willis looking out the parlor window. Others claim they've seen the children. Just glimpses of them, wild and ragged, flitting through the woods or standing by the gate late at night. Chelsea thinks they're evil, wicked, dangerous, just like Miss Willis. She says she'd never sleep if she lived on the farm. It's way too scary, everyone thinks so. Even her brother, who's not afraid of anything.

I didn't tell her I'd been inside the house, and I didn't tell her I'd seen Miss Willis. I had a funny feeling Diana didn't want me blabbing about the ghost. It's kind of a secret, even though I never promised not to tell. Even Dad doesn't know about Miss Willis.

So I just said in this really casual way, "Oh, I've never seen a thing. Your brother must be making that up to scare you."

Of course, down deep inside, I was so scared I couldn't look Chelsea in the eye. Sometimes I try hard to believe Dad's right about me imagining stuff, and that's all Miss Willis was—a figment of my imagination. But if Chelsea's brother and his friends have seen Miss Willis—well, then, she must be real.

And I never knew about the two kids going missing. Maybe that's why the policeman said I shouldn't be wandering in the woods by myself.

As for the ghosts of the kids, I guess Chelsea's brother saw Diana and Georgie running around in the woods the way they always do. I'd better tell them to be more careful or they'll be caught and then there'll be real trouble.

Oh, Dee Dee, I just had the strangest thought—I've got goose bumps all over. What if Diana and Georgie are the ghosts! That couldn't be, could it? I've touched Diana plenty of times, and she's just as solid and real as I am. So's Georgie. Of course, Miss Willis looked pretty real, but I bet if I'd touched her she wouldn't have been solid. Brrr—not that I ever want to see her or touch her!

I haven't seen Diana since the day we went inside the old Willis place. I think she's probably mad at me for dragging her in there. I can't really blame her. It was so stupid. I must have been crazy that day.

I haven't seen Miss Willis, either, thank goodness. I'm hoping she's gone back to being dead, resting in peace or whatever. But sometimes I swear I hear someone playing a piano. It's always the same thing—the Moonlight Sonata over and over again. I tell myself it can't be Miss Willis, but who else could it be?

Dad's never heard it, so naturally he thinks it's my imagination or maybe a car's radio as it goes past the farm. Which is ridiculous beyond belief. The road's too far away to hear car radios no matter how loud they are. And why would it always be the same music? I swear, Dee Dee, sometimes I worry I'm losing my mind. I wish I'd never gone inside that house! Nothing's been the same since.

I miss Diana. She might be a little strange, but she's much more interesting than Chelsea—who's not very smart and never reads a book unless her teacher makes her. She can do better cartwheels than I can, though, and she loves to show off her backbends. She wants to be a cheerleader. Not me. I'm going to be an Olympic champion—if I can just get better at backbends and cartwheels.

I really need to talk to Diana. She ought to know people have seen her and Georgie on the farm. I think I'll go to those houses across the highway and look for her. Maybe if I apologize again, we can make up and be friends like before. I could teach her how to do cartwheels and backbends and we could practice together and soon I'd be better than Chelsea.

Love, Lissa

Later the very same day

Guess what, Dee Dee? I went to those houses like I said I would. It was a long walk, but it was a sunny day and not too cold. It's a nice neighborhood. Lots of trees and a pretty little pond with a path that goes around it. I saw ducks and geese, mothers with strollers, people walking their dogs, joggers, some boys riding bikes. I wished Dad and I lived there. I noticed a house for sale, which I plan to tell him about.

But I didn't see Diana or Georgie. After a while I went up to a group of kids sitting on a little dock. They looked friendly, so I asked them if they knew a girl named Diana or her little brother, Georgie.

They said no, they'd never heard of them. I talked to them a long time, but they were absolutely positive Diana and Georgie didn't live in their neighborhood. They said they knew everybody with kids. No one was homeschooled. Everybody went to public school—except one boy named John, who went to St. Mary of the Mills.

What do you make of that, Dee Dee? It's very odd, isn't it? Now I have more questions than ever for Diana, the mystery girl. Or is she just a compulsive liar? I read a book once about a girl like that—she made up stories all the time to impress people. Take Miss Willis, for instance. Diana must be lying about her. Like I said, how can somebody hate you if they died while you were still a baby?????? Nothing about that girl makes sense!

Love, Lissa

Chapter 13

A few days later, Georgie and I were perched on a branch in our favorite tree. Without *Lassie* to read, I'd fallen back on *Clematis*. I had a feeling he wasn't listening to anything but the sound of my voice, a comforting background noise as meaningless as a cicada's song.

Annoyed, I gave him a sharp poke in the side. "You haven't heard a word I've said."

Startled from his thoughts, Georgie looked at me. "Do you ever get tired of being twelve, Diana?"

I closed *Clematis,* keeping my place with my finger. Oddly enough, it was a subject I'd given some thought to lately. I supposed it had something to do with meeting Lissa. She'd be thirteen next year, then fourteen, fifteen, and so on. Someday she'd probably get married and have children. But I'd remain twelve. Year after year after year. Just as Georgie would remain eight.

I reached up to stroke Nero, who was now entering his fifteenth year. He was showing a few signs of age, a white hair here and there in his coat, a certain stiffness in his gait.

He was one of a long line of cats we'd owned, each growing old and dying, leaving us to find a new one.

"Sometimes," I admitted.

"I was trying to figure it out," Georgie said. "In real life, I'd be almost seventy now. It's hard to be sure when you never have a proper birthday."

"I'd be seventy-two." I laughed. "That's old enough to be Lissa's grandmother. Isn't that funny?"

Georgie didn't laugh. His face solemn, he gazed past me, across the brown fields to the bare trees beyond. "I get so bored doing the same old things over and over and over again. Fish. Catch tadpoles. Climb trees. Swim in the pond. Wade in the creek. We've explored every inch of the farm. There's nothing new to see, nothing new to do."

I tried to think of a good answer, but I couldn't. I was bored, too. "That's one reason I wanted to be friends with Lissa," I told him. "She was new and different."

Georgie frowned at the mention of Lissa, but he didn't say anything about her. Instead, he busied himself peeling loose bark from the tree. "Read some more," he said. "I like to hear your voice."

I hadn't read more than two pages when I heard a twig snap. In the woods, branches swayed, and dry weeds rustled. Georgie grabbed my arm. "She's coming," he whispered. "It's her. Miss Lilian."

We froze, terrified. Should we run? Or stay still and hope she wouldn't see us?

Before we'd decided what to do, Lissa stepped out from the bushes. MacDuff followed her. He fixed his attention on Nero, who lay draped over a branch, tail twitching, eyes on the dog.

"What do you want?" I asked. It was a rude way to greet her, but I was still mad about what she'd done.

Georgie scowled down at her. "Go away!"

Lissa ignored him. She seemed close to tears. "Please don't hate me, Diana." She held up *Lassie Come-Home*. "I brought this back. I thought maybe—"

"It's a dumb story." Georgie folded his arms across his chest and frowned at the sky. "I hate Lassie."

"Come on, Georgie," I said softly. "Let me finish reading it to you. You're bored stiff with *Clematis*."

He didn't say yes and he didn't say no, so I leaned out of the tree and Lissa handed me the book.

"He can have the bear, too." Lissa held up Alfie. I could tell it was hard for her to give him up.

Georgie refused to look at Lissa, but I sensed he wasn't quite as mad as he had been. I reached down for the bear and sat him on a limb near Georgie. He ignored Alfie just as he'd ignored the book, but if I knew Georgie, he was secretly pleased Lissa had returned them.

"Can I climb up there with you?" Lissa asked me.

I shrugged. "If you like. It's not my personal tree or anything. I don't own it."

She scrambled clumsily up the trunk and slung a leg over

the branch below mine. After she'd made herself comfortable, she said, "I have to talk to you about something, Diana."

I looked at her and waited. She seemed unsure how to begin. Finally, she said, "I'm taking a gymnastics class at the Y. This girl named Chelsea asked me where I lived, and when I told her, she said Miss Willis isn't the only ghost here. There are two children. They disappeared a long time ago. No one knows what happened to them. But people say they still haunt the farm."

I gazed at Lissa, envying her pretty face and her shiny hair and her right to live in the world as an ordinary girl. What would she say if I told her the truth about those two children?

"Chelsea says some teenagers came here one night and saw Miss Willis looking out the window of the front parlor," Lissa went on. "They've seen the children, too. Just glimpses of them in the woods or at the gate. They say they're evil spirits."

I bit the inside of my cheek to keep from smiling. Teenagers often sneaked onto the farm to drink beer and smoke and kiss each other. Georgie and I loved to sneak up to their cars and make scary sounds. It was hilarious to see them start the engines and roar away, terrified. We'd been doing it for years, so it was no wonder kids talked about us. We were famous, I guessed.

"Have you ever seen the children's ghosts?" Lissa asked.

I caught Georgie's eye. He had his hand over his mouth to stifle his laughter. I knew he loved the part about our being evil spirits.

"No." I kept my voice as low as hers and tried to sound scared. "Are they dangerous?"

"I don't think so," Lissa said slowly. "They're just children."

"Children can be just as wicked as old ladies." Georgie swung by his knees from his branch, his face inches from Lissa's.

She backed away from him. "You'd better be careful. If you fall, you could break your neck."

"And die?"

"Maybe." Lissa glanced at me, as if she were unsure what to make of Georgie's behavior.

Georgie hung there, his face red, and laughed. Suddenly, he let himself fall. He hit the ground and lay sprawled in the weeds like a broken doll.

Lissa screamed and covered her face.

"He's all right," I told her. "Look."

Slowly Lissa uncovered her eyes. Georgie sat ten feet below, laughing up at her. He'd knocked the feathers in his hair crooked, but otherwise he was unscathed.

"That was so stupid," Lissa shouted, angry now. "You could have killed yourself!"

"Could I?" Still laughing, Georgie stood up. "What if I'm already dead? What if I'm a ghost?"

I wanted to tell him to stop before Lissa guessed the truth about us, but he was in one of his moods. He'd quit when he felt like it. I gave him a warning look, which he, of course, ignored.

"You're crazy." Lissa's voice was still shaky from the sight of Georgie plummeting out of the tree.

"*Boooooo!*" Georgie made a scary, google-eyed face at her and ran off. Nero and MacDuff watched him go. The cat remained on his branch and the dog remained on the ground, as if neither wanted to yield to the other.

"Your brother hates me." Lissa looked at me sadly. In a low voice she added, "Maybe you do, too."

"No." I flipped through *Clematis,* ruffling the pages like leaves. "But I don't see how we can be friends."

"Why not?" Lissa leaned toward me, her face earnest. "I told you I'm sorry. I promise I'll never go near that house again as long as I live."

I sighed and continued to flip the pages. "That's not why we can't be friends. There's so much you don't know about Georgie and me, stuff you'd never understand or even believe."

Lissa studied me intently, her forehead furrowed beneath a tumble of dark hair. "I know more than you think," she said slowly. "Yesterday I walked to those houses across the highway. I was looking for you. After a while I met some kids by the pond."

She paused to look at me closely. Unable to meet her eyes, I pulled a crimson leaf from a branch and twirled its stem in my fingers.

"They told me you don't live there," Lissa went on. "They know everybody, but they've never heard of you. Or Georgie."

"So? I told you we're not allowed to have friends." I shredded the leaf as I spoke. "I don't know them, either."

Lissa inched closer, till her face was inches from mine. "Want to hear what I think?"

I slid out on the limb until it dipped beneath my weight. My mouth felt dry. Had Lissa guessed the truth?

"I think you live right here on the farm," she said. "Like squatters. Maybe your parents are hippies or survivalists or even fugitives. Maybe they belong to a weird cult. I don't know and I don't care. You're my friend. That means your secrets are my secrets, too. I'll never tell anyone the truth about you—or your parents. Especially not Dad."

I shifted my position and the limb swayed. If only everything were as simple as Lissa thought.

"The thing is—" I cut myself off and stared past Lissa at the brown field and the house beyond. With most of the trees' leaves gone, I could see the roof and tall chimneys. How could I explain myself to an ordinary girl like Lissa?

"What's the matter, Diana?" She reached out to touch my

hand. "I can keep a secret. Do you live in one of the old barns? Or—"

"It doesn't matter where we live," I said slowly. "We won't be here much longer." As soon as I spoke, I knew it was true.

Lissa's eyebrows rose, giving her face a tense, worried look. "Is it because of me? Did your parents find out we're friends?"

I shook my head and felt the heavy weight of my braid shift. "No, it's not because of you. Or your dad. It's time to go, that's all."

"Do you want to leave?" she asked softly.

"Sort of." I fingered my braid. It was beginning to loosen, and I supposed I needed to redo it. "We've been here for ages."

"Lucky you." Lissa sighed. "Dad and I never stay anywhere long."

"Lucky," I echoed softly. If only she knew.

"But where will you go? If it's not too far, maybe we could still see each other." Lissa's face brightened.

I watched a long loose line of geese zigzag across the sky. Their loud cries rang out like the barking of dogs. They were leaving, too. "I think it will be much too far for us to see each other."

Lissa looked at me sadly. "Well, we can always write. And then maybe someday—"

I shook my head. "No. We won't be allowed to tell you where we are."

Lissa looked down at her feet. "More rules, I guess."

"Yes."

Lissa sighed. "Can you at least tell me when you're leaving? Tomorrow? Next week, next month?"

"I'm not sure." I listened to the thoughts in my head and tried to put them into words. "Georgie and I have to do something first."

"What do you mean—do something?"

"You ask too many questions, Lissa." I didn't know the answer myself. Not yet, at least. Exasperated, I tossed the books out of the tree. Grabbing a branch, I swung after them and landed on my feet as lightly as Nero.

Lissa looked down at me. "I'm scared to jump from here," she said. "It's too high. I could break my leg."

"Then climb down," I said impatiently.

I watched her make her way from branch to branch until she was low enough to drop to the ground. "You and Georgie must have rubber bones or something," she said. "I'd never have the nerve to jump that far."

"We've been jumping out of trees since before you were born."

Lissa laughed as if I were joking. "Oh," she said suddenly, "we forgot the bear." She pointed at Alfie, still perched on his branch.

"Don't worry," I said. "Georgie will come back for him and the books."

Lissa shook her head, still puzzled by my brother's behavior. "I hope you don't leave for a long time," she said. "I'll really miss you, Diana."

Maybe I'd miss her. Maybe not. She might fade like a forgotten dream after Georgie and I left. Who knew what we'd remember?

We crossed the field to the trailer. A curl of smoke rose from the chimney and the smell of soup met us at the door. Mr. Morrison looked up from the pot he was stirring and smiled. "Well, well, look what the wind blew in," he said cheerfully. "You're just in time for a big hot bowl of chicken soup with noodles, made from scratch, the best you ever tasted."

"Yum." Lissa sat at the table and patted the chair beside her. "Sit here, Diana. Dad is the world's greatest soup chef."

Before I could protest, Mr. Morrison set down two bowls and fixed a third for himself. The fragrance reminded me of my mother's soup. She'd made it from Miss Lilian's leftovers, thick and hearty, a treat for all of us, served with chunks of homemade brown bread and cheese.

I pushed the chair back and stood up. "I'm sorry, I can't stay. I have to go home. I promised Georgie—"

"But can't you eat your soup first?" Mr. Morrison asked. "Or bring Georgie back here for lunch? You look like you could use a nice hot meal."

"No, thank you." I edged away. "I really can't stay. I'm sorry."

"Some other time, then," Mr. Morrison said, his face as worried as Lissa's. "The soup's always on, and you're more than welcome to join us for a meal. You and your brother need to put some meat on your bones. You're so thin and pale, both of you."

"Dad," Lissa began, obviously embarrassed by her father's words. He'd meant well, I supposed, so I interrupted her.

"Thanks. That's very kind of you, Mr. Morrison." I opened the door and cold air rushed in. "But Georgie and I have all the food we need."

Safe outside, away from their questions and concerns, I ran with the wind across the field. Being with real live people was just too hard.

I found Georgie in the shed. With Alfie on one side and Nero on the other, he was leafing through *Lassie,* studying the pictures. A shaft of autumn sunlight lit his hair and face. He *was* pale, I realized. And thin. Surely he hadn't always looked so fragile.

"Read some more, Diana." Georgie held the book up. "Here's where you left off."

Grateful for something to do, I took the book and began chapter eleven, "The Fight for Existence." The picture showed Lassie, all bones and wet fur, running along with a dead rabbit in her mouth. I knew the dog had to eat, but I wished the artist hadn't shown her intended meal.

Georgie huddled beside me, listening intently to Lassie's struggle to survive her long journey from Scotland to England. He held his breath when she fell sick; he was angry when she was falsely blamed for killing sheep and almost shot, scared when she was captured by dogcatchers, and glad when she escaped.

At the end of chapter seventeen, "Lassie Comes over the Border," Georgie finally let me stop and rest my voice. Lassie was in England at last, safe for a while with a kindly old man and woman who planned to keep her forever.

"They won't, though," Georgie said as I closed the book. "Lassie's not home yet."

"No, she still has a way to go and a few more adventures before she's done."

Georgie lay back on his blankets and gazed out the shed door. It was dark now, and the moon had risen above the trees. It floated there, as big as an orange, dimming the stars but lighting the earth.

"How about us, Diana?" Georgie asked softly. "How far do we have to go before we're done?"

"I don't know." I stared across the silvery field at the black line of trees on the other side. A wind blew up. Branches creaked and swayed. Dried weeds rattled. Nero uncoiled from Georgie's side and stretched, his back arched like a Halloween cat's. He went to the door and peered out, ears pricked.

Georgie turned to me, his face fearful. "Nero hears something," he whispered.

"A mouse," I whispered. "That's all."

We both watched the cat. His body was tense; his tail lashed. He began a deep, vibrating growl.

The wind blew harder. All around us, trees and weeds and tangles of underbrush rustled and sighed and moved. A dry grapevine tapped against the wall. The tin roof rattled as something struck it. The shed's old timbers creaked. Dark clouds raced across the sky, veiling the moon and altering the shadows.

In the doorway, Nero hunkered down. His growl changed to a fierce song, its notes rising and falling along with the wind.

"It's not a mouse." Georgie clung to me. "It's Miss Lilian, she's come for us."

I shut my eyes and held him as tightly as I could. "No, it can't be her," I whispered into his hair. "It just can't."

But in my heart I knew he was right. Miss Lilian was out there in the dark, searching for Georgie and me, eager to punish us for the pranks we'd played on her.

Chapter 14

"Diana," a voice howled from the shadows, "Georgie, it's no use hiding. I'll find you wherever you are!"

The moon shot out from behind a cloud, and there she was in the field, brandishing a cane, her white hair blowing in the wind. Georgie and I stumbled to our feet.

I took my brother's hand. "Quick, out the back way!"

We plunged through a small door in the rear of the shed. With Nero racing ahead, we fled through the woods, tripping over roots and ducking branches. Brambles caught our hair and tore our clothing. But nothing stopped us or even slowed us down. We ran like rabbits fleeing a fox, like deer fleeing a hunter, like mice fleeing an owl, leaping, dodging, practically flying through the underbrush.

"Is she coming?" Georgie cried at one point.

"I don't know." The wind made so much noise we couldn't hear anything but branches thrashing over our heads.

We slid down the bank of the creek and into the ravine where we'd hidden Lissa's bike. It still lay there, rusty now, half submerged in water. We splashed past it and burrowed into a small cave, our favorite hideout. There in the darkness we crouched with Nero and listened. Miss Lilian's voice mingled with the wind's howls. Gradually her calls faded away into the night, and the wind died down.

Georgie cried with relief. I rocked him in my arms as I had for so many years. When his breathing quieted and he stopped sobbing, I lifted his face and looked into his eyes, as brown as a shady pond after rain. "She's gone," I said. "She didn't get us."

"But she'll be back," he said tearfully.

"Yes," I said slowly, "but we'll get away from her again. She'll never catch us."

"She did once," Georgie reminded me.

"We're smarter now." I crawled to the mouth of the cave and looked out. The night was still except for the distant rush of traffic on the highway. "She won't trap us again."

We slept in the cave that night. In the morning, I sneaked back to the shed and retrieved our belongings—our blankets and books, the flashlight, the penknife, and Alfie. Although I kept every sense alert for her presence, I didn't encounter a trace of Miss Lilian. Perhaps she couldn't leave her house in the daylight.

When I returned to the cave, Georgie was sitting at the entrance, braiding vines and leaves into his hair.

"For camouflage," he said. "You should do it, too."

I smoothed the long braid hanging over my shoulder. "I don't care to look like a savage."

"Suit yourself." Georgie finished his task and looked at me. "Do you think it's safe to leave the cave?"

"I didn't see a sign of her." I squatted down beside him. "Maybe she only comes out at night."

Georgie frowned. "I hope you're right."

I watched him poke at the dirt with a stick. "Do you ever have funny thoughts?" I asked him.

"Funny?"

"Odd," I said. "Odd thoughts."

"What do you mean?"

"Remember how the rules came into our heads and we knew them without anyone telling us what they were?"

Georgie kept his head down and scratched harder with the stick. He was writing his name, one of the few things he recalled from school. "Yes," he said slowly, "how could I forget?"

"Well, lately I've had a new thought. It came the same way. No one told me. All of a sudden it was in my head, like colors and smells and sounds, things that don't need words."

"It's about leaving, isn't it?" Georgie didn't look at me. He was adding finishing touches to his name—little curlicues on each letter.

"Do you have the same thought?"

"Yes," he said. "But we have to do something first."

I nodded. "Do you know what it is?"

With a gesture of impatience, he rubbed out his name. "I think it's got something to do with her."

"Miss Lilian?"

"Yes." He dropped his voice to a whisper. "And with our bodies. Our real ones."

I shivered. "Someone should bury them and say the right words so we can rest—"

"I know that." Georgie scowled, signaling he'd heard all he wanted to hear about our bodies and their burial.

We sat beside each other silently and watched the last leaves spin down from the trees. The creek was filled with those that had already fallen. Shades of red, yellow, and brown, different shapes and sizes. Some were caught in eddies, others lodged among the stones, and a few raced on the current on their way to a larger stream.

Georgie reached out over the water to prod a few leaves loose with his stick. He watched them sail around a bend and turned to me. "Will you read some more of *Lassie*? I want to know how it ends before we leave."

"We're coming to a sad part," I warned him.

"Just read," Georgie said. "I'm used to sad parts. And so are you."

I began at chapter eighteen, "The Noblest Gift—Freedom." Lassie had recovered her strength. Every afternoon just at the time school let out, she began pacing the floor of the little cottage. The old folks tried to make her happy. They treated her well, they fed her and petted her and loved her, but still she wanted to leave, she had to leave.

Georgie pressed against me. "Do they let Lassie go?"

I read on. The old woman opened the door. She and her husband followed Lassie to the road that ran by the cottage. They watched Lassie hesitate. They wanted to call her back, but they knew the dog had to leave. The old woman told Lassie it was all right. If she had to go, why, go she must.

Georgie breathed out a long sigh. We were glad Lassie was on her way but sorry for the old man and woman, left alone in their cottage, too sad to eat their evening meal. The old man offered to bring home another dog, a small one, but no dog could take Lassie's place. So he suggested a cat instead, "the bonniest little cat ye ever did see."

Georgie glanced at Nero sitting nearby, licking his paws and scrubbing his face. "I bet it was a big black cat just like Nero."

At my brother's urging, I kept reading until I finished. The story ended just as Georgie had hoped. After a few more struggles, Lassie made it home and met Joe at the school gate as she used to. This time Mr. Carraclough didn't make Joe return the dog to the duke. Instead, he nursed Lassie back to health. In the end, the duke hired Joe's father to run the kennel, he let Joe keep Lassie, and Lassie had puppies.

Georgie grinned. "I wish I could hear it all over again."

Chapter 15

Later that day, I walked to the trailer. It was too cold for Lissa to do her schoolwork at the picnic table, but I hung around for a while, hoping she'd come out. I liked Mr. Morrison, but I wasn't in the mood to pretend to be a normal girl.

After several minutes, I gave up and knocked at the door. Maybe Mr. Morrison was busy in his room, writing his book.

But no, he opened the door and gave me a big smile. "Why, Diana," he said, "come in. You must be freezing in that thin blouse and skirt. And look at your feet. Where are your shoes?"

I hesitated on the threshold, heedless of the wind blowing through the open door. Oh, why did he and Lissa have to ask so many questions?

Before I could change my mind and run back to the woods, Mr. Morrison took my hand and drew me inside. "I promise not to give you any more chicken soup," he said with a laugh. "I didn't realize you were a vegetarian."

A vegetarian—he and Lissa had an amazing ability to

come up with explanations for my odd behavior. I supposed the truth was too fantastic for them to guess.

Lissa came out of her bedroom and mumbled a greeting. She was pale. Anxious.

"Miss Grump got up on the wrong side of the bed this morning," Mr. Morrison told me, winking to show he was teasing Lissa. "She hasn't had one nice thing to say."

"I brought your book back." I handed *Lassie* to Lissa. "We finished it this morning. Thanks for letting us borrow it."

Lissa took the book as if it no longer interested her and laid it on a table beside the couch. I couldn't think of what I'd said or done to make her mad, but something was obviously bothering her.

"And *Clematis,* if you still want to read it." I laid the tattered book, its pages warped from the shed's dampness, beside *Lassie.* "It's a good story. With a happy ending."

"Thanks." Lissa opened it, releasing a slight odor of mildew. "I like the illustrations. They're so quaint."

Mr. Morrison leaned over to take a look. "'By Bertha and Ernest Cobb,'" he read. "Copyright 1917. That is an old book. Where did you find it?"

Inwardly I groaned at yet another question. "In a used-book store," I lied.

Mr. Morrison nodded and handed Lissa MacDuff's leash. "Why don't you two take MacDuff for a walk," he suggested. "You could both use some fresh air."

While Lissa snapped the leash to MacDuff's collar, Mr. Morrison turned to me. "That silly dog kept Lissa and me awake all night, barking his fool head off. I don't know what's gotten into him. All I heard was the wind, howling up a storm out there in the woods."

"It was really blowing hard." I made an effort to sound like an ordinary person talking about the weather, but I knew what MacDuff had heard. And so did Lissa. Miss Lilian must have wandered all over the farm in the dark and the cold, searching for Georgie and me.

Suddenly anxious to leave, Lissa grabbed her jacket from a hook near the door. "Do you want to borrow a sweatshirt, Diana?"

"For heaven's sake, yes," Mr. Morrison answered for me. "She must be freezing."

To satisfy them, I pulled Lissa's thick red sweatshirt over my head and followed her and MacDuff outside.

"Don't let Diana blow away in the wind," Mr. Morrison called to Lissa.

Lissa gave him one of those looks I'd given my father when he'd said something embarrassing. She didn't answer him or speak to me. I'd never seen her so quiet.

After we were out of Mr. Morrison's sight, Lissa turned to me anxiously. "It wasn't just the wind last night, was it?"

"No," I said.

Lissa drew in her breath. "She called your name and

Georgie's name. Even with my head under the covers, I could hear her."

"I told you she'd come after us," I said.

"But why?" Lissa asked, genuinely puzzled.

Instead of answering, I kept walking, head down, scuffing leaves out of my path. If only I could tell her the truth. She might believe me now. After all, she'd seen Miss Lilian. She'd heard her voice in the wind. She must realize ghosts exist.

"I was with you in the house," Lissa went on, her voice shaky. "She should be after you and me, not Georgie. He wasn't even there."

I looked at her. She was close to tears. "I couldn't sleep a wink last night," she said.

"She's not after you," I insisted. "She won't hurt you."

"I hate this place," Lissa went on as if she hadn't heard me. "I told Dad we have to leave, we can't stay here, but he won't listen to me. He acts like I'm a baby afraid of the dark."

Lissa sat down on a boulder at the edge of the field and began to cry. I huddled beside her, sorry she'd been drawn into Georgie's and my troubles. Indifferent to our worries, Mac-Duff followed his nose into the weeds, roaming in circles around us, happy to be outside smelling wonderful smells.

Glad for each other's company, Lissa and I pressed closer together. She shivered despite her warm jacket.

A thick white cloud cover hid the sky, and the air smelled of snow —the first of the year, earlier than usual. My father would have said Mother Goose was about to shake the feathers out of her pillows.

I gazed across the field toward the house. A gust of wind blew through the treetops, making a mournful sound. The air filled with flying leaves. A thought formed in my head, then another and another. They came from nowhere, just the way the rules had. Suddenly, I knew exactly what to say to Lissa. And, more importantly, what not to say.

"Do you remember telling me about those missing children?" I asked her.

She looked at me. She'd stopped crying, but her eyes were red and wet. "The ones Chelsea says haunt the farm?"

I nodded. "What if I told you what happened to them?

"Those children vanished a long, long time ago. How could you know anything about them?"

I leaned closer, forcing Lissa to meet my eyes. In a whisper, I told her the words I heard in my head. It was almost as if someone else was speaking—a ventriloquist, maybe, using my voice. "When we first came here, Georgie and I found an open window in the basement. We used to climb inside and explore the house. It was scary, just like it is now. Creepy. We played the piano, we went through the closets, we stole books and clothes."

"You said it was against the rules to go in the house," Lissa reminded me. "Weren't you scared your parents would find out?"

"In those days, our parents weren't as strict as they are now. We didn't have as many rules."

MacDuff interrupted me with a series of loud barks. He ran to Lissa and sat close to her, whimpering. We both looked across the field, to the trees and the house beyond. We saw nothing, but the dog's behavior made us uneasy.

Lissa bent over MacDuff and stroked his sides. "What's the matter, boy?" she whispered. "Do you see something?"

The dog rested his head on Lissa's knee and gazed at her in a way that made me think of Lassie. He thumped his tail and grinned, as if he'd merely been seeking affection.

I touched Lissa's arm to regain her attention. "One day Georgie talked me into exploring the cellar. We'd been afraid to go down there because it was so dark, but Georgie borrowed a big flashlight."

Lissa continued to pet MacDuff, but she was paying close attention to me.

"We found a door in a dark corner of the cellar. It was bolted shut," I whispered. "And when we opened it—"

Suddenly, Lissa drew back, alarmed by something in my voice. "No, I don't want to hear any more."

She covered her ears like Georgie used to, but I pulled her hands away and held them tight. Somebody had to know where Georgie and I were and who had put us there. Somebody had to see to our burial. Otherwise, we'd be prisoners on the farm forever. These were the new rules. I knew them just the way I'd known the old rules.

MacDuff looked at us uneasily, as if he didn't like the way I was holding Lissa's hands.

"We opened the door," I went on relentlessly, spinning the lie as I talked, speeding up the story. Since it was partly Lissa's fault that the old woman was loose, she might as well be the one to fix things. "Two children were huddled together on the floor. Dead."

I saw our bodies as they'd been when Georgie and I began our new lives. Like the empty shells of locusts left on tree trunks, they were no longer needed. But they had to be found, they had to be buried.

"Stop it, Diana," Lissa whispered. "You're scaring me."

"It's true. Miss Lilian locked the children in and left them there to die. No one knew about the room. No one ever found those children."

"No," Lissa sobbed. "No, that's horrible, no one would do something so cruel."

Once more she tried to free her hands. I held them tighter. MacDuff growled.

"She was crazy," I cried. "She hated us!"

"Us?" Lissa stared at me. "You said 'us.'"

"I mean Miss Lilian's ghost," I corrected myself. "She

hates Georgie and me because we know she killed the children." My story told, I let go of her hands. MacDuff relaxed and rested his head once more on Lissa's knee.

"Those poor children," Lissa whispered. "Those poor, poor children. And their parents—they never knew what happened to them. Oh, Diana." She was crying again.

"Tell your father, Lissa. Make him believe you. Those children must be buried properly. They can't rest till they're in their graves."

"Is that why their ghosts are still here?"

"Yes." It was true. I knew it. Once our bodies were found and buried, Georgie and I would be free to go—wherever it was we were going.

Lissa slid off the rock. "Come with me. Help me tell Dad. He'll never believe me."

"No, I can't." I jumped down beside her, anxious to settle things, to start them moving. "You have to do it yourself."

Lissa hesitated. "But, Diana, he'll be mad, he'll know I went in the house, he'll—"

I gave her a push toward home. "Go," I cried. "Go right now. Run! And be sure and tell him who killed them."

The first flakes of snow had begun to fall, melting where they landed. MacDuff raced in circles, his mouth open in a lopsided grin, snapping at the flakes. Lissa called to him, her voice shrill.

I watched the two of them vanish into the woods. The

old rules had changed, fragmented, broken into bits. Telling Lissa had been the right thing to do. I was sure of it.

But I'd changed everything for Georgie and me. The life we'd shared for so many years was about to end.

What would replace it?

THE DIARY OF LISSA MORRISON

Dear Dee Dee,

Last night the wind blew really hard and MacDuff started barking like he heard something outside. Dad said it was teenagers again, sneaking out here to drink beer, but oh, Dee Dee, I heard a voice calling Diana and Georgie. It's Miss Willis—her ghost, that is. Dad went out to chase the teenagers away. I told him not to. It wasn't teenagers, it was—but he left before I could say what it was. I stood in the open doorway, watching him, scared of what might happen. There was no car, no teenagers, just Miss Willis hollering in the dark. Dad came back inside, fussing about pranks, but he never once said he heard anyone calling.

Diana and Georgie are lucky to be leaving this horrible place. If only Dad and I could move away, too.

Today, I asked Diana why Miss Willis was after them. I'd asked her before, but she'd never really answered. This time she told me the truth. Those children who disappeared died in the cellar of the Willis house, and their bodies are still there. Miss Willis locked them in a secret room and left them there to die. Diana and Georgie found the bodies. Diana thinks Miss Willis is after her because she knows who killed the children.

Diana spoke so calmly, but I felt like I might throw up or faint. How could something that horrible happen to two children? I wanted to cover my ears and run away, so I'd never have to see the farm again. Why did I drag poor Diana into that house? Why did she let me? She should've stopped me, she should've told me what was in the cellar. If I'd known, I wouldn't even have sat on the terrace.

Diana said I had to tell Dad about the bodies, I had to make him believe me. The children must be buried properly. Otherwise, they'll never rest in peace.

So I ran home, just when the snow was starting, and I told Dad.

At first he didn't believe me. He said Diana must be pulling my leg. But I begged him to go to the cellar and see for himself. Finally, he said, Okay, okay, but nothing will be there. This is ridiculous, and so on and so on and so on while I was crying and shaking and terrified.

Finally, he took his keys and a flashlight and left with MacDuff.

I was all alone. I wished Diana had come home with me like I'd asked her to. The wind was blowing and the snow was falling and now it was sticking, not melting like before. It was almost dark, and I was scared Miss Willis would hurt Dad. What if she locked him in the room with the children's bodies? I hadn't thought of that when he left.

So I put on my parka and my boots and gloves and hat and went out to look for him. The wind blew the snow in my face, cold enough to take my breath away. "Dad!" I called. "MacDuff!"

No one answered. I walked on, still yelling for Dad and Mac-Duff.

Oh, Dee Dee, when I was close enough to see the house, Miss Willis stepped out of the trees and stopped in front of me, blocking the way. She wore the same raggedy gray silk dress, and her hair blew, as white as snow itself.

"Diana!" she screamed at me. "Diana, stop running from me!"

"I'm not Diana," I cried, but she reached for me as if she hadn't heard me. Her hands closed tight on my wrists, colder than the snow, stronger than steel.

"Diana, listen to me! Don't run away!"

This close, her face was the color of bone. Her eyes were sunken and shadowy, but they glittered with rage. She shook me fiercely. "Where's Georgie?"

"Let me go," I sobbed, "let me go. I'm not Diana!"

She tightened her grip and leaned closer to me. Her breath smelled like her house, old and dank. The wind tugged at her dress. "I know you," she whispered. "You're the girl who let me out, the one who changed everything. Should I thank you? Or curse you?" She paused a moment and grinned. "Or should I lock you in the cellar?"

Somehow, I broke free and ran toward the trailer. Behind me, I heard a horrible witchy laugh. "Stupid girl," she cried. "Did I scare you?"

I didn't know if she was chasing me or not. I was scared to look back. Screaming and crying for my father, I flung open the front door and kicked it shut behind me. Exhausted, I collapsed and lay on the floor, too scared to move.

After a while, I heard someone thumping on the door. I covered my ears and stayed where I was. It was her, I knew it was. She'd come to lock me in the cellar.

"Lissa, let me in!" Dad yelled.

I got to my feet and staggered to the door. I was scared to open it. What if Miss Willis was still there? Would she hurt Dad? My hands shook so much I could hardly turn the knob.

He stepped inside, bringing cold air with him. I threw my arms around him and kept on crying. He patted my back and smoothed my hair, but I could feel him trembling.

"Oh, Lissa, Lissa," he whispered. "I found the room just where Diana said it would be. It was terrible . . . terrible."

His voice broke and he sank down on the couch. He looked awful, Dee Dee, like he'd just seen the most horrible thing you can imagine. I think he was as scared as I was. And close to tears, too, Dee Dee, which frightened me even more. I hadn't seen my father cry since Mom died.

"How could anyone do something like that?" he asked in a shaky voice. "Those poor children, those poor little children, left there like that, locked in, abandoned."

He hugged me so tight I could hardly breathe. When he let me go, neither of us said anything. We just sat there. I guess we were in a state of shock. The wind was blowing so hard the trailer shook.

I was sure I heard Miss Willis out there. And so did MacDuff. He kept pacing around, whimpering and whining the way he does when he's nervous about something. Dad told him to lie down, but he wouldn't.

After a while, Dad said I looked exhausted. He was right. I was so tired I ached all over like I had the flu. He made me go to bed and fixed me tea and sat down beside me while I drank it. He'd made it with lemon and honey and it tasted so good.

Then he called the police and told them what he'd found in the cellar. I listened to his voice, still shaking as he talked. He said it was no wonder the children were never found. Someone had piled boxes and old furniture in front of the door to the room.

There was a pause and then Dad said, "Yes, I agree. It must have been Miss Willis. Who else could have done it?"

After he hung up, he came back to my room and sat with me for a while. It was dark by then, and the snow blew past my window in a pale blur. My room looked safe and cozy, but I didn't feel all that secure. Not with Miss Willis out there looking for Diana and Georgie. I hoped they felt safer than I did. But I doubt it.

"The police will be here early tomorrow," Dad said. "They'll see to it that the children are properly buried."

That made us both feel a little better, I think.

I tried to tell Dad what I knew about Miss Willis, but he said, "Hush, hush, let's not think about that old woman anymore. She'll give us nightmares for sure." He hugged me and kissed my forehead and tucked me under the covers, all tight and snug and warm.

MacDuff came to my room and jumped up on my bed. Dad usually chases him off, but tonight he said he could stay. MacDuff is the best old dog in the world, but even with him right here beside me I'm still scared.

I wish the wind would stop. I wish it was morning. I wish we *lived in one of those nice little houses across the highway. I wish Diana lived there, too, and we went to the same school and took gymnastics together.*

Most of all, I wish those children hadn't died in that cellar. They must have been so scared, Dee Dee.

Love, Lissa

Chapter 16

When Georgie and I woke in the morning, the falling snow hung like gauze between the mouth of the cave and the ravine, blurring rocks and trees, earth and sky. The only sounds were the gurgle of the creek and the wind, now a soft murmur.

Georgie peered out at the snow, at least a foot deep already, and laughed. "No school today!"

It was a joke of long standing now, left from the time when we'd actually gone to school and celebrated days off.

Nero sat at the cave's entrance, his displeasure evident. He looked at me as if to say, "What sort of bad joke is this?"

"The little mousies are safe from you today," I told him.

Nero twitched his tail and stalked to the back of the cave. There he snuggled in the blankets and watched the snow through slitted eyes.

"Do you think the police will come in this weather?" Georgie asked me.

The night before, I'd told him what I'd asked Lissa to do.

I'd thought he'd be angry, but he'd listened calmly. "It's the first step." He'd tapped the side of his head. "I feel it here. You know, like the rules."

Now the two of us watched the snow fall: barefoot, bare-legged Georgie, half naked, with feathers in his hair; me with my long braid, and Lissa's sweatshirt over Miss Lilian's flowered skirt. Neither of us knew what to expect next or how to prepare. Without saying a word, we left the cave and walked through the snow toward the house. We had to see the police come. We had to watch them go, too. We had to be sure.

We met Lissa and MacDuff halfway down the driveway. She ran to us, her face pale despite the wind and snow. "I've been looking for you," she cried. "I was scared she might have gotten you last night."

Lissa didn't need to say the name. We knew who she meant. "We heard her," I said. "She came close a few times."

"Old witch," Georgie muttered. "She won't get us again."

Lissa breathed a sigh of relief. "She caught me last night. She thought I was you, Diana."

For once, Georgie looked at Lissa without sneering. "How did you get away?" he asked.

Lissa shook her head. "I guess she wanted Diana, not me."

"I bet you were scared," Georgie said, some of his old scorn returning.

"I was terrified." Lissa began crying. "Dad went to the house to look for the children's bodies, and I got scared and followed him. That's when she grabbed me. She was so horrible. . . ."

I hugged her as if she were a little child, years younger than I was. "I told you she wouldn't hurt you," I whispered.

"Did your father find the children's bodies?" Georgie asked.

Lissa nodded. "Just where Diana said they'd be. He called the police. They're supposed to come today." She looked around doubtfully. "But with all this snow . . ."

I drew in my breath and took Georgie's hand. There was no turning back now. Whatever I'd begun the day I met Lissa had to run its course.

"I see them." Georgie pointed down the driveway.

The three of us ducked behind a tree. Led by a police car, a hearse made its way slowly toward us.

"It's the same one that took Miss Lilian away," Georgie said.

"How do you know that?" Lissa asked.

"All hearses look the same." I spoke quickly to keep Georgie from saying anything else. "That's what he means."

Georgie frowned, but he didn't argue as I'd feared he might. Instead, he gave Lissa a sassy look, which she ignored. The two of them would never be friends.

The police car passed us, its lights flashing. An officer in the passenger seat was drinking coffee from a paper cup. The other was intent on driving. Behind them the hearse slipped and slid, but the driver managed to keep it on the driveway.

"Where do you suppose they'll take us?" Georgie asked me.

"The police aren't going to take you anywhere," Lissa said. "They've come for the children's bodies, not for you."

Georgie drew closer to me. "You think you're so smart," he told Lissa scornfully. "But you don't know anything."

"Shh," I warned him as softly as I could.

The wind whipped Lissa's hair around her face, and she hunched her shoulders against the cold. From the looks of her, she was scared and cold—and very unhappy.

The silence between us grew. We were alone in the trees. The police car and the hearse had vanished around a bend in the drive. Every now and then, we could hear tires spin in the snow.

"Let's not fight any more, Georgie," Lissa said. "I'm sorry for all the dumb things I've said and done. Dad says I'm too prickly. I guess he's right."

I looked at my brother. "You're sort of prickly yourself, you know."

"So what if I am?" He scooped up a handful of snow and hurled it at a tree—*splat*. "I could've thrown it at you," he told Lissa with a grin, "but I didn't."

Lissa smiled. "It's good you didn't," she said. "My dad taught me how to make a really hard snowball."

Georgie touched my hand. "Come on."

With MacDuff bounding ahead, we plodded on through the snow until the house was in sight. Georgie pulled me behind a huge oak. Lissa hid with us, pressed beside me.

The hearse and the police car, its lights still flashing, were parked by the front steps. The tall double doors stood open. While Mr. Morrison talked with one of the police, the men from the hearse maneuvered a gurney up the rotting steps. Excited by the commotion, MacDuff ran to Mr. Morrison. One of the policemen patted him.

"Are you going to watch them bring the bodies out?" Lissa whispered. I had a feeling she wanted to leave.

Georgie nodded, but I touched his arm. "Let's go."

"Why?"

"Because it's morbid to stay here and watch," I told him.

"Don't you want to be sure they find us?"

I glanced at Lissa, but she was edging away toward the warmth and safety of the trailer. She hadn't heard Georgie.

"Please, Georgie," I whispered. "Watch what you say. Do you want Lissa to know everything?"

He shrugged. "It doesn't matter anymore."

"I'm going to the trailer with her," I said. "Please come with us."

Georgie didn't answer. Nor did he move. His attention

was fixed on the house's open doors and the darkness beyond.

I left him there and ran after Lissa. "Wait!"

Behind me, the policeman's voice droned on. He was saying something about ghosts, old mysteries, Miss Lilian's role in the children's disappearance. With every step I took, my back prickled. I was tempted to look over my shoulder, but whatever came out of that cellar was best not seen.

From the high gray dome of the sky, a hawk dove toward the field not far from the drive. In a second he was flying upward again, a mouse in his talons.

Lissa glanced at the hawk and shuddered. "I hate this farm."

"Hawks have to live," I said.

"It's not just the hawk and the mouse," Lissa said. "That's just plain old nature. I mean ghosts and dead children and crazy people—things that give me nightmares. I want to leave, like you."

I followed her into the trailer. "Do you want hot chocolate?" she asked.

"No, thanks."

"How about peanut butter cookies?" She held out a plate. "Dad and I made them this morning. Don't they smell delicious?"

I shook my head. "Thanks, but I'm not hungry."

Lissa sat down at the counter. I took a seat beside her. "I

guess your parents don't allow you to eat sweets," she said.

"That's right." I toyed with a pencil lying on the counter, spinning it idly this way and that. It was hard to think of anything but the cellar and what the men from the morgue were doing down there.

Lissa fixed herself a cup of cocoa and ate a few cookies. I breathed in the aroma. It was almost as satisfying as actually eating and drinking.

"Let's play checkers," Lissa said. "The board's all set up."

I followed her to the sofa. The checkerboard lay on the coffee table, ready to go. "Red or black?" Lissa asked.

"Black." I picked up a checker and rolled it in my fingers. Maybe a game would take my mind away from the cellar.

Lissa won easily. Not because she was a good player. I made sloppy moves, I overlooked traps, I let myself be cornered and captured.

"What's wrong, Diana?" Lissa asked.

"Nothing." I gathered up my captured men and began setting up the board for another game.

"You're miles away," she insisted. "I can tell by the way you're playing."

I sat back and studied the checkers lined up on the board, so orderly, so perfect. Had the men put the bodies in the hearse? Was Georgie still watching? I shouldn't have left him there all by himself in the snow. I should have made him come with Lissa and me.

"It's the children in the cellar, isn't it?" she asked. "You're thinking about them."

Lissa jiggled the board accidentally, and I nudged a checker back into position.

Undiscouraged by my silence, Lissa moved closer to me. "How did you keep it a secret so long?"

I sighed. "There was no one to tell."

"Your parents—you could have told them."

"I wish to heaven I could have." I slid away from Lissa and gazed out the window across the room. Bare trees blew in the wind. Georgie was out there, small and thin, his hair full of leaves and feathers, watching, waiting.

"I can't believe your parents are as strict as you say." Lissa slumped on the couch and propped her feet on the coffee table, further disturbing the order of the checkerboard.

Silently I leaned forward and moved the pieces back to the center of their squares.

"Oh, Diana." Lissa sighed. "Sometimes I feel like I don't know you at all."

"You don't," I said.

She stared at me, speechless for once.

Mr. Morrison chose that moment to open the door. MacDuff followed him inside, wagging his tail, shaking snow off his fur.

Lissa jumped to her feet, scattering the checkers in her haste. This time I ignored them. What did it matter, anyway?

"Did they take the children away?" she asked.

Mr. Morrison blew his nose. "They've made arrangements to bury them at Mount Holly."

"Do their parents know?" Lissa asked.

Mr. Morrison shook his head. "It's such a sad situation. The children's parents are both dead. No uncles, no aunts, no living relatives."

I got to my feet, my chest tight, my legs weak. "They're dead?" I asked. "Mother and Daddy both?"

Lissa looked at me oddly, but I was too upset to wonder why. All I could think of was what her father had just said, his voice so calm, his manner so ordinary.

"That's what the police told me," he said. "They're buried at Mount Holly. At least the children will be with them now."

I covered my face with my hands. All this time, I'd pictured Mother and Daddy alive somewhere, waiting for news of us. I hadn't considered the weeks, the months, the years as they'd rolled past. As Georgie had said, it was hard to keep track of time without birthdays and holidays.

I felt a hand on my shoulder. "Now, now, Diana," Mr. Morrison said softly. "I don't blame you for crying, but it happened long ago. Try to think of it as a story you read in a book."

"You don't understand," I whispered. At that moment I wanted him to put his arms around me as if I were his child, his daughter. I wanted him to comfort me, to stroke my hair. I wanted to tell him everything about Georgie and me and Miss Lilian and the terrible thing that happened to us. I wanted him to know who those bodies belonged to. Instead, I shrugged his hand off and edged away from him, closer to the door, closer to escape. "It's not a story," I said. "It's true."

Lissa eyed me solemnly, full of curiosity, but for once she had no questions.

"Of course it's true," Mr. Morrison said, beginning to sound uncomfortable. "I was only trying—"

"I know," I said. "It's okay." I'd reached the door. My hand was on the knob. I turned it.

"Don't leave, Diana," Mr. Morrison said. "I'll fix you tea, hot chocolate —"

"Dad." Lissa took her father by the arm. "I think Diana wants to go home."

With MacDuff between them, Mr. Morrison and Lissa stood in the doorway and watched me leave. "Find Georgie," Mr. Morrison called. "Bring him back here. We can watch a video. Eat supper. I make a great vegetarian chili."

"No," I said. "I'm sorry. I can't."

I turned my back on the open doorway and the warmth inside and ran across the field toward the woods.

Chapter 17

I found Georgie in the cave with Nero, huddled under a pile of blankets, his dirty face tear-streaked.

"Georgie, Georgie." I threw myself down beside him and held him tight. "What did you see? What did you hear?"

He cuddled close to me, as much in need of comfort as I was. "They came outside with the gurney," he whispered. "They'd zipped us—our bodies—into black bags. Oh, Diana, the bags were so small. I guess all they found were—"

"Hush." I covered his mouth with my hand. "I told you not to watch."

Georgie pushed my hand away. "You have to hear this part, Diana. It's about Miss Lilian."

I lay back, propped on my elbows, and let him go on.

"The police were talking," Georgie told me. "One said it might've been an accident, but the other said the door was bolted from the outside. That meant someone had locked us in, he said—and who else could it have been but that crazy old woman?"

"It's a shame nobody figured that out sooner," I said. "Miss Lilian got away with killing us. She never went to jail, she was never punished."

"It's not fair." Georgie scowled. "It's not fair, Diana!"

I pulled the covers up under my chin. The fading light of day shone through the cave's opening, barely illuminating the darkness around us. "Did the police say anything else?" I asked.

Georgie shifted his position to see me better. "Mother and Daddy are dead," he said in a low voice. "But I'd guessed that already. Hadn't you?"

"I always hoped they'd come back for us someday," I told him. "I guess that's silly, but, well, I wanted it to be true, so I—" I pressed my lips together and tried not to cry.

"They're going to bury us with Mother and Daddy," Georgie said, as if to console me. "We'll all be together, Diana."

I wasn't consoled. I wanted to be with Mother and Daddy again, but not in a graveyard. I wanted them to be here on the farm, the way we were before the bad thing happened.

Outside, twilight darkened into night. The wind blew harder, soughing in the treetops. Far away, from the direction of the house, came the faint sound of a piano. Miss Lilian's favorite piece, the *Moonlight* Sonata, floated through the darkness, eerie, distorted, out of tune. I pictured her at the piano, back in the days when its mahogany gleamed and every note was true. Her hands struck the keys, her head moved to the music's rhythm, her thin body swayed. I stood in the doorway, watching, hearing her mistakes, yearning to push her aside and play the piece properly. She looked up and saw me. Her face twisted in anger, and she slammed the piano lid shut. "Get out!" she yelled. "Get out!"

Pushing the memory away, I burrowed deeper under the covers, hoping to block the sound of the piano. Beside me, Georgie slept quietly, Lissa's bear clasped to his chest. Nero came closer, turned around once or twice, and curled between us, purring as if he hoped to comfort us. But there was no comfort without Mother and Daddy.

The next thing I knew, Georgie was shaking my shoulder. "Diana," he whispered. "Something's outside the cave."

I rose to my knees, listening for sounds in the darkness outside. I heard nothing, but Nero's back rose and his tail puffed to twice its normal size. The cave filled with his eerie growling song.

"It's her." Georgie clutched my arm, his nails biting into my skin. "It's Miss Lilian."

We crept to the cave's entrance and peered into the night. The wind shook shadows across the snow, confusing my eyes.

Then I heard what Georgie had heard, a voice calling,

rising and falling with the wind. She was in the woods, not far away, coming toward us.

"Run," Georgie whimpered. "Don't let her get us!"

I would have taken his hand, but he was clutching Alfie. The two of us darted out of the cave and slid down the snowy bank into the creek. She must not trap us again.

Through the woods, across fields and streams, uphill and down, we ran and she followed, calling us again and again. Our names echoed from bare trees, bounced back from the snow, became unrecognizable. Deer fled from the sounds of the chase, bounding through the snow in fright. A fox barked from a boulder and vanished into a thicket, fearful for his own safety.

Georgie and I came out of the woods behind the house. It sat on the hill above us, a dark shape crouched against the moonlit sky, its crooked chimneys rising like broken fingers from the roof. We ran across the snowy lawn spiked with dead weeds. I looked back. She was behind us, running as only the dead can run, tirelessly, her white hair wild and loose in the wind, her gray dress fluttering.

"Diana, Georgie," she cried, as if she knew no words other than our names. "Diana, Georgie!"

"Not there!" I grabbed Georgie's arm to steer him away from the house.

He looked at me, glassy-eyed with fear, as if he didn't know where he was or what he was doing.

Still holding his arm, I skirted the house and ran down the drive. The tracks of the police car and the hearse cast shadows in the snow. Like a ghost himself, the albino deer stood at the edge of the trees. He watched us for a moment and then vanished into the shadows.

Behind us Miss Lilian called, "Diana, Georgie! Diana, Georgie!"

On we ran. On she came.

At the end of the driveway we realized we could go no farther. We'd come to the fence between us and the rest of the world. I yanked Georgie to the right, planning to run along the fence, but he slipped in the snow and fell by the gate, pulling me down with him.

We scrambled to our feet, but we were too late. Miss Lilian had us trapped between the fence and a thicket of bushes and vines heaped with snow.

She was close enough for us to see her clearly. She was old, she was ill, she was thinner than ever. She stretched her bony hands toward us and chanted our names, "Diana and Georgie, I have you now. Don't try to escape. I've chased you more than enough!"

I thrust Georgie behind me. She mustn't get him, she mustn't hurt him. I'd protect him this time. "What do you want?" I cried. "Haven't you done enough to us already?"

She lunged at me, seized my arm, and pulled me close. Her cold fingers pressed my skin, chilling me to the bone.

"You've given me no rest, no peace. Not while I was alive. Not after my death. And now, now—"

"Leave my sister alone." Still holding Alfie, Georgie tried to pull me away from Miss Lilian. "You hurt us, you made the bad thing happen!"

"You!" She turned to Georgie, her face filled with fury. "You were always the bad one. Making faces at me behind your mother's back, teasing and tormenting me, stealing my things. Why, you have my bear right now. Give him to me!"

Georgie drew back, clutching Alfie. "This is my bear, not yours! Lissa gave him to me."

"Let us go," I begged her. "We can't harm you now."

"Oh, no." Miss Lilian held us both, her grip too strong to break. "I can't let you go. Not yet. We have old accounts to settle, the three of us."

Georgie and I clung to each other in dread. What accounts? Tweaking Miss Lilian's skirts, knocking pictures off the walls, breaking knickknacks, slamming doors, hiding her jewelry, taking her money—small things compared to what she'd done to us.

"Just look at you," she said suddenly. "Hiding on my farm like fugitives, one of you dressed in my clothes and the other wearing almost nothing but feathers in his hair. Filthy. Rude. Stealing and lying. You're a disgrace to your parents. To my parents. To society itself."

"It's your fault we're here!" Georgie cried.

Miss Lilian stepped back as if he'd struck her. "My fault? How dare you say such a thing? Nothing is my fault. Nothing!"

"Liar," Georgie retorted. "You know what you did."

"What happened was your own fault," Miss Lilian went on. "You deserved to be punished. Someone had to teach you a lesson. Your parents never raised a hand to you. They let you run wild. So the duty fell to me."

Too angry now to be afraid, I thrust my face into hers, daring her to harm me. "You chased us into the cellar and locked us in that room, and then you left us there—"

"To teach you a lesson," she repeated. "That's all I meant to do."

"A lesson?" I stared at her in disbelief. "You killed us!"

She released us then and began fidgeting with the string of pearls around her neck. "No," she whispered. "It was an accident. An unfortunate accident. Surely you realize I didn't mean to hurt you. I didn't mean to!"

Georgie brushed me aside and walked right up to Miss Lilian, storming with anger. "You're a murderer!" he shouted. "You should have gone to jail. They should have executed you!"

"I had a stroke," Miss Lilian shouted back. "A stroke! You upset me, my blood pressure shot up, I collapsed at the top of the cellar steps. Your mother found me on the kitchen floor, unconscious. Your father called an ambulance. They put a tube down my throat, they put something over my mouth. How could I tell anyone where you were? I was more dead than alive."

Miss Lilian smoothed her dress, touched her hair, wrung her hands nervously. "I was in the hospital a long time. Weeks, months, I can't be sure. I couldn't speak. Couldn't move. It's a wonder I didn't die." She toyed with the pearls, sliding them between her fingers one by one as if she were counting them.

She peered at Georgie and me, her eyes sharp. "When I finally recovered, what happened in the cellar seemed like a dream, a nightmare—not something I'd really done."

I stood in the snow, almost mesmerized by the soft *click, click* of the pearls, and tried to understand what I'd just heard. Miss Lilian hadn't meant to kill us. It was an accident. She'd had a stroke and gone to the hospital. While she was there, unable to speak, we'd died, Georgie and me.

"Why didn't you tell someone when you could talk?" I asked her.

Miss Lilian's hands strayed from her pearls to her hair and then to her dress, smoothing, twitching, tweaking, never still. "What good would it have done? You were dead by then."

"Our parents—" I began, but Miss Lilian interrupted, her voice shrill.

"I would have been arrested. Me—Lilian Eleanora Willis, the daughter of Judge John Willis, the granddaughter of an attorney, the descendant of one of the oldest families in Maryland. Can you imagine the disgrace?"

She touched her hair again, smoothed her dress, opened and shut her mouth, grimacing with the effort of finding the right words. "I lived to be almost one hundred years old," she went on slowly, close to tears now. "Every year was more miserable than the one before. All I wanted was to die and be done with it. But ten years after my death, I'm still here on this farm, as unhappy as ever. No rest, no peace. I've been punished long enough. I want to move on. It's time. Past time."

The old woman took a deep breath and looked toward the empty road beyond the gate, her face filled with longing. The moonlight fell on her gaunt face, darkening her eyes.

"Now you know the truth," she said. "Don't stand there like ninnies. Speak up. Say what must be said. Or, or—" Her voice dwindled and she began to fidget with her pearls again.

Words crowded into my head. I knew what must be said, I knew what must be done. But it wasn't easy.

While Georgie stood there, hugging his bear, I forced myself to take Miss Lilian's hand and look into her eyes. Her hand twitched as if she intended to draw it away, so I held it tighter, pressing the bones in her fingers.

"We've been angry with you for a long time," I told her.

"Afraid of you, too. But now I think we must forgive you. And you must forgive us."

Georgie snorted in surprise. "Why does she need to forgive us? What did we ever do to her that she didn't deserve? Everything's been her fault. Even before the bad thing, she was mean."

Without releasing Miss Lilian, I grabbed one of Georgie's hands. "Stop blaming her. She's old. Let it go. All of it. Everything."

Clutching Alfie with his free hand, he tried to pull away, his face sulky. I squeezed his hand. "If we don't forgive each other," I said, "we'll all be here forever. It's the last rule, Georgie. Can't you feel it?"

Georgie didn't look at me or Miss Lilian, but his hand went limp in mine. I watched the anger leave his face. Cautiously I placed his hand in Miss Lilian's. He didn't yank it away. Like Miss Lilian, he stood quietly.

"I'm sorry I locked you in the storeroom," Miss Lilian said to Georgie and me. It cost her a lot of effort to add, "And before—I shouldn't have treated you the way I did. Even though you—"

"I'm sorry I teased you and took your things," I said quickly, before she ruined her apology.

For a moment Georgie didn't speak. I squeezed his hand again, worried he was about to doom us to an eternity at Oak Hill Manor.

"I'm sorry, too," he finally managed. But he didn't look at Miss Lilian. He held Alfie tightly, as if he expected the old woman to snatch the bear away.

The farm was still. No owl hooted, no fox barked, no wind stirred the trees. Beyond the fence, the highway was deserted. Something was about to happen. We could sense it in the silence.

Slowly the moonlight brightened. It cast ink-black shadows across the brilliant snow. Half blinded, we drew closer together, unsure, a little afraid.

"Diana," Georgie whispered. "Look."

He pointed at the road. Two people walked slowly toward us, their faces indistinct, their forms shadowy despite the blinding light. Georgie pressed himself against me, and Miss Lilian held my hand tighter.

"Who are they?" Georgie asked. "What do they want?"

"It's Mother," I whispered, "and Daddy. They've come for us at last."

Georgie and I broke away from Miss Lilian and shoved the gate open. We ran out into the road, free at last from the farm and its rules.

Mother and Daddy hurried toward us, calling our names, eager to hold us once more. Georgie sprinted ahead. As he flung himself at Mother, I heard Miss Lilian cry, "Don't leave me! Take me with you!"

I came to a sudden stop halfway between the gate and my

parents and looked back. The old woman stood at the edge of the light, her arms stretched out to Mother and Daddy. "Please," she cried, "please, forgive me."

Mother turned to Daddy, her eyes full of questions. When he hesitated, I ran to him. "Don't leave her here," I begged. "She didn't mean to, it was an accident. She's sorry."

Mother looked at Daddy again. This time he nodded. Mother held out her hand. "Come with us, Miss Lilian."

I walked to the old woman. As I reached for her hand, I noticed Alfie sitting on the fence. I glanced at Georgie but said nothing. It was clear he no longer needed the bear.

Miss Lilian hobbled through the gate toward me. She looked back once, as though bidding Oak Hill Manor farewell forever.

Together, the five of us walked into the brilliance. It was as if we were entering the moon itself.

THE DIARY OF LISSA MORRISON

Dear Dee Dee,

I will never see Diana or Georgie or Miss Willis again. They are gone forever.

But before I tell you how I know that, I guess I should start with what Dad told me after Diana left.

Dad fixed hot cocoa for me and coffee for himself. Then he put the plate of peanut butter cookies on the table and sat down across from me. "The police told me the names of the children in the cellar," he said. "Diana and Georgie Eldridge. Odd coincidence, those first names, don't you think?"

It made me shiver all over because I had the same thought I'd had before about Diana and Georgie. Only now I knew it was true. Diana and Georgie were the children in the cellar. The bodies in the storeroom were their bodies. Suddenly, everything about Diana made sense, and I could hardly believe I hadn't figured it out earlier.

Which means ghosts are not at all what I imagined them to be. Not transparent, not spooky, not phantoms of the night, but real and solid, with shadows and everything—only they never get cold and they can't eat or drink or hurt themselves. You could sit next to a ghost at a bus stop and never know it. You could be friends with one and not even suspect. That's what I think, at least.

After Dad told me the children's names, I started crying. He tried to comfort me. "You're too sensitive to deal with all that's happened here," he said. "Maybe we should move, maybe I should find a different job. Go back to teaching, maybe. Would you like that? You could live in a neighborhood with other kids and have a more normal life."

I stared at him, amazed. "Do you really mean that?" I asked.

He said yes, he meant it. He'd been thinking about it for several days, and it seemed to him I needed more friends. He doesn't want me to spend so much time alone. It's not good for me, he says. Especially now, in light of all that's happened.

So he's going to start looking for a job and another place to live. I told him about the house for sale across the highway. He said he'd look into it, but it's probably too expensive.

In the meantime, I can start school in Adelphia.

Which makes me very happy, even though the farm doesn't seem so scary now that Miss Willis is gone.

BUT, DEE DEE, THAT'S NOT THE END OF MY STORY.

That night, Miss Willis began calling Diana and Georgie again. Even though I was afraid, I looked out the window. In the moonlight, I saw Diana and Georgie running across the field toward the driveway. Miss Willis was close behind.

I pulled on my boots and parka and sneaked outside. Stumbling through the snow, I ran after them. I didn't know what I was going to do, but I wished I'd brought MacDuff.

Miss Willis caught Diana and Georgie by the gate. I didn't dare go too close, so I couldn't hear anyone but Miss Willis, who ranted and raved loudly enough to wake Dad. She blamed everything on Diana and Georgie. It was their fault they died in the cellar. Not hers. How could she believe such a crazy thing? She locked them in; she left them there.

She had excuses for everything, but what she did was wrong—she should have told Diana and Georgie's parents. She made them suffer even more because they never knew what happened to their children.

Then an amazing thing happened, Dee Dee. Diana reached out and took Miss Willis's hand. She made Georgie take the other. He didn't want to. For once I was on his side. I would never have forgiven that horrible old woman. They all spoke in low voices. Oh, I wish I'd been brave enough to creep closer so I could have heard what they were saying.

Suddenly, the moon began to shine brighter and brighter. It almost blinded me. I've never seen a moon like that. It was absolutely supernatural. And terrifying. But beautiful, too. I crouched in the shadows, and waited to see what would happen next.

The next thing I knew, Diana and Georgie ran out the gate and into the road. I heard Georgie call his mother and father. Miss Willis stood by herself, watching them go. Then she stretched out her arms and cried, "Don't leave me!"

Diana turned and looked back at Miss Willis. The moon shone right through her. She held her hand out to the old woman—the very person who had killed her and her brother.

I ran toward Diana. I had to say goodbye, I had to tell her I'd never forget her, but before I reached the gate, she was gone. And so was Miss Willis.

The moon dimmed and shone with an ordinary light, and I could see the highway stretching away, empty. Behind me, leading up to the gate, were three sets of footprints, four counting mine. On the other side, the police car and hearse had left their tracks, but not one footprint marked the snow on the road.

And then I saw something on the gate—my bear, just sitting

there as if he was waiting for me. Georgie must have left him for me. I picked up Tedward and rubbed my face against his soft fur. He smelled like Georgie, not quite clean but not really dirty.

I don't know how long I stayed at the gate, shivering in the wind, staring at the empty road and the moon high up in the sky as bright as a new dime. Did I think they'd return if I waited long enough?

No, they were gone for good. And they'd let Miss Willis go with them. Even after the terrible thing she'd done.

Finally, I got so cold I thought I'd freeze to death standing there by the gate. Feeling sad and lonely, I turned my back to the highway and started home. The wind made a racket in the treetops, but I didn't hear Miss Willis or her piano. No one watched me from the woods. The night was as ordinary as a winter night can be, and I was alone.

Well, not quite alone. Halfway home, who did I see but Nero, making his way toward me, lifting each paw daintily and giving it a little shake. He meowed as if to say he'd been waiting for me a long time and he was cold and hungry.

I picked him up. His purr rumbled against my chest and I buried my face in his soft, sweet fur.

"Well," I said, "I guess you're my cat now. So you might as well come home with me."

When I tell Dad Diana is gone (not where or how, just that she moved like an ordinary girl), I know he'll let me keep Nero. I just hope MacDuff won't mind. Surely he's used to the cat by now.

Oh, Dee Dee, I wish I'd had a chance to say goodbye to Diana. Every time I see the full moon, I'll think of her and wonder where she is. Happy, I hope. With her family in some beautiful place beyond the moon.

Maybe my mother is there, too. I wonder if she'll come for me some moonlit night a long, long time from now.

Love, Lissa